Blood Never Sleeps

Sarya knelt on the dusty roof, looking towards the DAESH sniper's position. Olan fired the PK one shot at a time, with Gulan feeding the ammunition belt. Barî, Keya and Soran contributed with their rifles, but it was obvious their target was just out of range, even for the PK. Sarya looked for a building closer to the sniper, but they were all half-destroyed and unable to be used. Only this house was intact enough, but it was just out of range. Just then Sarya sensed movement. She looked across the roof to the upstairs rooms of the house, where she saw three figures in semi-darkness. Keeping low out of habit, Sarya sprinted across a roof littered with spent cartridge cases. There she faced a YPG comrade, and two men wearing camouflage with body-armour and beige vests; no doubt with 'press' on their backs. One of those men held a professional-looking camera.

"Rojbash Havel," Sarya greeted the comrade.

"Rojbash Komutan Sarya," he replied. "I have Daniel and Brett from Vice Television."

Sarya shook hands with Daniel, and then with Brett the cameraman. "Do you speak English?" she asked in English.

"We do," Daniel said.

"Okay," Sarya said while she gathered her thoughts. "We have a DAESH sniper under fire, but he's just out of

1

range so I was going to call an airstrike. Come with me and I will show you."

Sarya led the way towards the parapet, and knelt beside Olan still firing.

"The DAESH sniper is there," she said while she pointed out his building. "I will call for the strike, and we will keep firing so the sniper won't get suspicious and leave his building."

Daniel nodded while Sarya told Olan what she was going to do. He nodded while he kept at one shot after the next. Sarya sat cross-legged on the dirty roof and took the tablet computer out of its cover.

"This tablet has a satellite image of all DAESH positions, real time," Sarya said. She used her fingers to zoom the image and centre it. "We are here," she said while the cameraman filmed over her shoulder. "The DAESH sniper is there. Now I will call for the airstrike." She pulled her radio from her sleeve pocket and pressed the transmit button. "Komutan Sarya Goran from Team Martyr Agir," she said in Kurdish. "Airstrike on DAESH sniper, coordinate seventeen-twelve," she said.

"Airstrike on DAESH sniper, coordinate seventeen-twelve," the operator confirmed.

Sarya put her radio away, and moments later heard the roar of a jet closing. She stood to watch while the cameraman filmed the jet flying low and fast, until the aircraft suddenly climbed vertically, straight up into the sky. Moments later there was a massive explosion, and the sniper's position was obliterated by a cloud of concrete dust. The rest of the team celebrated, while Sarya told Daniel they got the sniper. The cloud of dust and debris slowly cleared to reveal a heap of rubble and smashed concrete. Nobody could have survived that.

"This is a good outcome," Sarya said in English to Daniel.

"How many are left?" Daniel asked.

"Maybe four-hundred," Sarya said. "But they will fight to the last." She slid her tablet into its cover, and slipped her trusty AK47 over her shoulder. "Now we must go. There's another sniper in the next street. Perhaps this time we will get him with our rifles." Olan already had the PK over his shoulder, while Gulan was burdened with the RPG and her backpack. Barî, Keya and Soran were also ready.

Daniel shook Sarya's hand. "Thank you so much, Commander Sarya," he said.

She nodded while the cameraman, Brett, shook her hand.

Sarya led their team into the three-storey house, very dark after the intense sunlight outside, down the stairway, and outside to a dirty, dusty street. She trudged over rubble while looking out for IEDs and grenade drones, and sensing the camera filming from behind.

3

Blood Never Sleeps

by

Mark Morey

Mark Morey

http://markmorey.blogspot.com

Copyright ©

978-0-6480647-8-7

Published In Australia

March, 2018

Other Works by Mark Morey

The Red Sun will Come - June 2012

Souls in Darkness - August 2012

The Governess and the Stalker - July 2014

Maidens in the Night - September 2014

One Hundred Days - September 2015

The Last Great Race – April 2016

The Adulterous Bride – October 2016

No Darkness – March 2017

In Our Memories – November 2017

Map of Syria

Parties Involved with the Syrian Civil War

Islamic State (IS)

This group was founded in 1999 by Sunni Jordanian Abu Musab al-Zarqawi as *The Organisation of Monotheism and Jihad*. Following the 2003 invasion of Iraq by America, Britain and Australia, al-Zarqawi and *The Organisation of Monotheism and Jihad* undertook suicide attacks on Iraqi Shia mosques, Iraqi civilians, and Iraqi government institutions. In October 2004, when al-Zarqawi swore loyalty to Osama bin Laden and al-Qaeda, he renamed the group *The Organisation of Jihad's Base in Mesopotamia*. In July 2005, al-Qaeda outlined a four-stage plan to expand the Iraq War. This plan included expelling US forces from Iraq, establishing an Islamic authority as a caliphate, spreading the conflict to Iraq's secular neighbours, and clashing with Israel.

On 7 June 2006, a US airstrike killed al-Zarqawi, who was succeeded as leader of the group by the Egyptian militant Abu Ayyub al-Masri. On 13 October 2006, the group declared the establishment of the *Islamic State of Iraq* **(ISI)**, with Abu Omar al-Baghdadi as emir.

After the death of Abu Omar al-Baghdadi in April, 2010; Abu Bakr al-Baghdadi was appointed the leader of ISI. Al-Baghdadi replenished the group's leadership by appointing former Iraqi Army Officers, and Iraqi Intelligence Service

Officers, who, like he, spent time imprisoned by the US military. In July 2012, al-Baghdadi declared the start of a new offensive in Iraq, aimed at freeing members of the group held in Iraqi prisons. Violence in Iraq began to escalate in June 2012, primarily with car bomb attacks.

In 2013 following a split with al-Qaeda, ISI became involved with the Syrian Civil War. On 8 April 2013, al-Baghdadi announced a new name *Islamic State of Iraq and the Levant* **(ISIL)**, sometimes being known as the *Islamic State of Iraq and Syria* **(ISIS)**. The Arabic acronym of this is **DAESH**. On 29 June 2014, ISIL proclaimed itself to be a worldwide caliphate with Abu Bakr al-Baghdadi named caliph, and the group renamed itself *Islamic State* **(IS)**. As a Caliphate it claims religious, political and military authority over all Muslims worldwide.

Democratic Union Party (PYD)

Formed in 2003 in Kurdish-dominated Northern Syria, the **PYD** is the leading political party for that area known as Rojava. In 2004 the PYD formed a self-defence militia known as the *People's Protection Units* **(YPG)**. For many years the PYD suffered persecution from the ruling Arab Socialist Baath Party, including imprisonment and torture of PYD activists. Following the outbreak of the Syrian Civil War, the YPG was dramatically increased in size, and included a new brigade, the *Women's Protection Units* **(YPJ)**, for female volunteers. The YPG and the YPJ subsequently formed the backbone of the *Syrian Democratic Forces* (**SDF**), which went on to achieve success against Islamic State (IS or DAESH).

The PYD follows teachings of imprisoned Turkish **PKK** leader Abdullah Öcalan. For more than 30 years the PKK has conducted a war of armed conflict against Turkey, and as a result the PKK is recognised as a terrorist organisation by Turkey, the United States, the Europe Union, NATO, and several other countries. Turkey has stated that the PYD is the same as the PKK, and Turkey is currently supporting an invasion of the canton of Afrin inside Syria.

Chapter One

Vache leaned against the balcony rail with a mug of coffee in his hand, while he watched crowds streaming past. He had a good view from their second-floor apartment of men and boys shouting and cheering, some carrying banners and flags; looking like supporters for a major football match. But that wasn't a football crowd. In towns and cities all over Syria on Friday the 22nd of April, 2011; crowds were calling for the overthrow of the Assad regime. And in Raqqah, crowds were moving towards Naeem Roundabout as the assembly point for their protest.

Vache sipped his coffee just as Erna came alongside. "Do you want to go to the protest?" she asked.

"This is only for men and boys," Vache said.

"Assad is a friend of Armenians."

"As a Shia in a Sunni-majority country, he needs support of minority groups like Christians."

"I can never understand Shia and Sunni. A Shia man can marry a Sunni woman and that's no problem. Both families are happy, and wishing the happy couple a long life together with many children. Or they live and work side-by-side with no issues at all, but once it gets to politics, then that's a big problem."

For whatever reason, Shia and Sunni was an inevitable part of Arab politics.

"Something's going to come out of this," Vache said. "Protests have gone from demanding democratic reforms and the release of political prisoners, to overthrowing the government."

"Change is inevitable," Erna said. "Look at these past few months. Tunisia in December, then Algeria, Jordan, Oman, Egypt. Who would have thought Libya would overthrow Gaddafi?"

"Social media...," Vache said, and Erna smiled. "Dictators can control conventional media, but they can't control Facebook and Twitter."

"Yes; without the internet there never would have been an Arab Spring, or the protests today."

"Assad is as brutal and corrupt as any dictator, and he won't go without a fight."

"Unless the army deserts him."

Vache sipped his coffee. "True," he said.

"It was stupid, no, arrogant to torture and kill that seven year old for writing anti-government graffiti on a wall."

That was true too, and the catalyst for nationwide protests that day. "I think we should keep a low profile, because it's best to be on the winning side." He finished his coffee and put the mug on the table. "With this chaos, surgery is cancelled for the doctor today," Vache said. "I wonder what we can do to pass the time?" he asked rhetorically.

12

Erna laughed, and punched his shoulder.

"Are you interested?" Vache asked Erna.

"Always," she said.

He hugged and kissed his beautiful wife, before leading her inside and sliding the door closed behind.

* * *

It was chaos at Naeem Roundabout, with crowds pushing, shoving and jostling. In his nineteen years, Adnan had never seen anything like that. Never seen anything remotely like that. With his cousin Fadi, Adnan made a banner demanding Assad be exiled, while many others had banners of their demands. And to show their patriotism many, including Adnan's father, held Syrian flags. Men with loud hailers called for the end of the dictatorship and the exiling of the dictator, with free and fair elections to follow. The crush slowly moved along broad al-Mogmaa Street towards al-Rasheed Park. There was much chanting and cheering as the crowd filled the street with a mass of humanity. Maybe a hundred-thousand, and all wanting the same thing. Adnan was elated to be part of such a historic day. Surely with so many united in Raqqah, and so many more united across Syria, change would come. Surely that day was the beginning of the end of the brutal and corrupt leadership of his great country.

* * *

On a cool, spring morning, they gathered at Memorial Park.
Hundreds and hundreds of teenagers, and young men and
young women too. Sarya felt the buzz of excitement while
she gathered with her friends Gulan, Dila and Medya. From
what she could see almost all of the older children from her
school, the girl's school, and many teenagers from the co-
educational school were there. For once they could protest
against Assad and his anti-Kurdish policies, without fear of
violence or fear of a massacre. Mohammad Wali must have
been proud of this protest of youth in Amûdê.

Sarya unfurled the banner she and Gulan made over
previous nights; written in Kurdish and demanding that
Kurdish language and Kurdish culture be respected within a
new Federation of Syria. Writing Kurdish or speaking their
language in public was against Arab-Syrian law, or even
having a Kurdish name like Sarya was against their laws. Like
most Kurds, Sarya was registered with an Arab name, which
was never used. Others had banners, where the most
important issue was citizenship. The vast majority of Syrian
Kurds were stripped of Syrian citizenship decades before,
despite Syria being their land for many generations.

Their protest march gradually sorted into order, with
Sarya and Gulan proudly holding their banner finished in the
colours of the Syrian Kurdish flag: yellow, red and green. For
once they could march and not be subjected to violence and
brutality, because the regime was losing control. There were

14

too many protests that day, organised through the internet and social media, for Assad to deal with.

They marched through the city centre, along streets lined by their parents, cheerfully singing songs in Kurdish and defying anyone to stop them. Hundreds and hundreds of young people clustered together, many with banners and flags, on a day of defiance. Unfortunately their march was over far too quickly, but many had filmed their demonstration on smartphones as a reminder of a great day in the city of Amûdê.

Sarya bid her friends farewell, and rather than find her parents in the confusion, she headed home. Amûdê was flat, so flat that water towers were needed to provide water pressure to the city, although there were rolling hills in the near distance. Houses and commercial buildings were mostly simple rectangular with flat rooves, and built of concrete bricks. Uniformly sand-coloured, with only those water towers, the television transmission tower, and the mosque minaret rising above. Sarya let herself into their three-bedroom home to find Mama and Papa waiting. Her Papa hugged her.

"This was a great day and I'm proud of you," he said.

That made Sarya feel even more elated, if such a thing were possible. "This is just the beginning," Sarya said. "Freedom is coming, and for us in Rojava that means a democratically confederal state within a federation of Syria."

"Like you've been taught in school?"

He knew, because he was the headmaster. "Like we've been taught in school," she echoed. "Here in Rojava, we'll unshackle ourselves from capitalism and the patriarchy, and live a life of collectivism."

Mama rustled Sarya's hair. "Before collectivism we must eat, and as much as your father believes in equality, he doesn't know how to cook! So can you help me please?"

Today was too important, and too good an opportunity. "Papa, you can help," Sarya said. "You can make our tea, and you can carry our dishes too."

Papa chuckled. "That's collectivism," she said.

"Yes it is."

Three in the kitchen was somewhat crowded, but worth it. Soon they were sitting on the floor of the living room with dishes spread before them, and Papa's tea to accompany their Friday lunch.

"It's a pity Daran missed today," Mama said.

Sarya's older brother Daran was away studying law. "Perhaps he protested in Damascus," Sarya offered.

"That will be the day," Papa grumbled.

"Elind!" Mama exclaimed.

"Perhaps he protested in Damascus," Papa said, but Sarya knew he didn't mean that.

"Now that we've protested across Syria," Sarya said. "Where does this go from here?"

Papa sipped his tea. "I truly don't know," he said. "It'll take more than a day of protest to unseat Bashar al-Assad, and many days of protests could drive him to take action. We shall see."

Sarya sipped her tea. She knew they'd done the right thing, and she hoped that was the start of a new order for her and for her people. But how that new order came about would only be known in time.

Chapter Two

Vache kissed Erna on her cheek before they separated: she towards the hospital where she managed nurses in the outpatients department, and he to his general practice. It wasn't a long walk, about ten minutes along al-Mogmaa Street and past 50-year old concrete apartment buildings and office blocks, many with shops, banks, restaurants and cafes at the ground floor; not yet open at that time of the morning. He worked in the wealthier district of Raqqah, and they rented a spacious and expensive apartment nearby. Raqqah had the reputation of the most boring city in Syria, and for a man raised in bustling Aleppo; that was mostly true. But now that Vache was married, living in a boring city didn't matter so much, and Raqqah had offered a great opportunity. Just as he was finishing his internship at Aleppo University Hospital, where he met Erna, his father told him the Armenian doctor at Raqqah was retiring and the practice was for sale. Raqqah wasn't so far from family and friends in Aleppo, and as a bonus Erna obtained a more senior position at the National Hospital. So Raqqah it was, with its bustling city centre located between Naeem Roundabout and the iconic Clock Tower Roundabout, and also around the corner from there. Further away were ramshackle-looking small apartment buildings with ground floor shops and small businesses; all squashed together and crowding busy streets; with modern and spacious apartments further away again. At the edges of Raqqah were bleak outskirts of small industry and cheap houses, and this area was dusty in dry weather and muddy when it rained. The highlight of the city was the broad Euphrates River to the south, and especially Bridge Park on the far banks of that river. When they had children, which would happen in time, mingling with the many families who enjoyed Bridge Park on weekends would be wonderful.

There were many faults with the Assad regime, father and son, but their greatest achievements were the promotion of sectarianism and the rejection of Islamic fundamentalism. That made cities like Raqqah, peaceful and tolerant homes for all. The greatest weaknesses of the Assads had been autocratic rule through an almost permanent state of emergency, sometimes brutal repression of the Kurdish minority in the north of the country, and presiding over economic stagnation, made worse by drought over the past few years. Many Syrians had struggled for the basics in life for many years, and that was boiling over. Syrians were less concerned about democracy and more concerned about three meals a day, a roof over their heads, and a little extra to cover emergencies. And when Hafez al-Assad and then Bashar al-Assad ruled completely and totally for decades, it was easy to sheet home the blame for Syria's economic malaise.

Double glass doors automatically slid open as Vache approached, and he entered a lobby of polished granite, marble and mirrors. Mirrors everywhere, reflecting his 190cm build, wavy black hair, and dark grey Armani suit. To one side of the ground floor was his practice, where through the doorway he greeted his receptionist Rima. Then into his consulting room, where Vache prepared himself for the first of his patients. The laid-back and easy-going lifestyle of Raqqah was reflected by the people who lived there, and almost universally his patients were friendly and affable. Vache was pleased to have bought a prosperous practice, and pleased that Raqqah was such a pleasant place to live and work.

* * *

As expected, Ranim waited at al-Rasheed Park. When Adnan closed she stood and he kissed her cheek. Ranim was a genuinely attractive girl: fair skin, dark hair not often seen; dark eyes; small and slim, and shoulder-high to he, who was average build for a man. But more important than her pleasing looks; Ranim had a good heart. Today she wore blue slacks and a light blouse also in blue, ideal for a pleasant, spring evening, with a dark blue hijab draped over her head and across her shoulders. Adnan wore blue trousers too, but with a black shirt. He took her hand and they headed deeper into the park.

"How was your day?" Ranim asked.

"Some days are steadily busy, where you don't get a moment to yourself," Adnan said.

"That cafe will be yours one day."

"It will, but I need a job that pays better in the meantime."

"I know, but your father needs you to work there."

That was the problem for Adnan. As the only son he had family duties, but there was another issue. "How can I marry you on what I earn?"

"We're young and that will come in time."

It was true they were young, but Adnan couldn't imagine his life without Ranim. Right now if they were married they could, but unmarried they couldn't, and sometimes that was hard.

Adnan held Ranim's small, soft hand while they walked in silence. Just appreciating her company. "How was school?" Adnan asked.

"School was good," Ranim said. "But I'm looking forward to finishing next year."

"Do you have plans?"

Silence for a moment. "Maybe marriage with a good and decent man."

Adnan nodded his head, and he needed to get out of that cafe.

"Hey brother!" a loud voice shattered the silence. Adnan saw his friends Abdul, Bakir, and of course Hardi with the loud voice. They closed and greeted each other with cheek kisses, except for Ranim of course.

21

"Making the most of a nice evening, brother," Hardi said while clasping Adnan around his shoulders.

"Yes we are; away from family," Adnan said as a subtle hint.

"Yes, yes; of course. A couple needs time together."

"That's right."

"Would you like something to eat or drink?" Bakir asked.

"Aah...," Adnan said, not wanting to go that far.

"It's just that Abdul and I have been conscripted, and soon we'll be leaving."

Adnan understood. All eighteen year olds with brothers were conscripted to the army, which was one bonus for Adnan. His job at the family cafe was far better than two years in the army.

"Let's find somewhere nice for your farewell meal," Adnan said.

"I protested against that tyrant on Friday, and now I'm forced to fight for him," Abdul grumbled.

Adnan put his arm around Abdul's shoulder. "I'm really sorry for you," he said.

"I know you are."

"When are you two getting married?" Hardi asked bluntly.

"We're young and there's plenty of time," Adnan said.

"Are you conscripted too?" Ranim asked Hardi.

"No; I have two sisters and no brothers," Hardi said.

They reached Church Street and headed towards the busy Clock Tower Roundabout. There were many cafes and restaurants there, including al-Rasheed which was quite classy. Hardi guided them in that direction, but Adnan didn't want to spend so much when there were cheaper restaurants around.

"You have good friends, and this will be a good night," Ranim said, and she always knew the right thing to say.

Adnan looked into her lovely eyes. "This will be a good night," he agreed, and he was sure it would be.

Chapter Three

Vache carefully disentangled his body before glancing at the clock; eight-ten on a Saturday morning. He stretched and looked into Erna's peaceful eyes.

"Good morning," he said quietly.

"Good morning," Erna whispered in reply.

After a time she rolled to her side of the bed, while Vache stretched before reaching for his phone.

"Ha!" Erna exclaimed.

"There's a lot happening at the moment," Vache said defensively.

"I know."

Vache opened the al-Jazeera app and scanned the news. A lot was happening for sure. For the past six months, protests for the overthrow of Assad had continued, often with the army responding, sometimes leading to street battles like those seen in other countries. Rocks, stones and Molotov cocktails, against water cannon and even bullets. The Syrian Army had split, with a large group of commanders and men forming the Free Syrian Army, which was battling the government army in what had become a civil war. Jabhat al-Nusra l'Ahl as-Sham, an offshoot of al-Qaeda, then appeared on the scene, perhaps from across the border in Iraq, and Jabhat al-Nusra was battling the Syrian Army as well. Jabhat al-Nusra attracted young Syrian men, no surprises given the high rate of youth unemployment, and as a reflection of the times, Jabhat al-Nusra advanced their cause through social media and YouTube. Recruitment of willing soldiers via Facebook and Twitter.

"How are things?" Erna asked.

"Same as last night," Vache said. "The major battle is the Free Syrian Army against the Syrian Army at al-Rastan."

"What about Jabhat al-Nusra?"

"They're not mentioned this morning."

Erna sat cross-legged. "I don't like their association with the terrorists al-Qaeda, and their ideology of an Islamic State under sharia rather than secular law. That's not for us."

"I don't like that either."

"Do you have any ideas?'

"Keep an eye on developments, and be prepared to leave if necessary. All we have is this rented, one bedroom apartment with our furniture, which is fairly basic, and the goodwill I purchased for the practice. That's not much, and we can start again if we need to."

"I've been thinking about that, but other places haven't struck me. Even though we're Armenian, we don't belong in Armenia. That looks like a different world, and they even speak a different dialect of Armenian to us. We do speak Arabic."

"We also speak English," Vache said.

"Arabia is our home."

25

"Jordan or Lebanon?" Vache asked

"Either, I think."

Vache wasn't so sure. "If we leave, it should be once only. Countries like Jordan and Lebanon can become unstable virtually overnight. And if things go bad here, they'll be flooded with refugees."

"Not so many doctors and nurses though."

That greatly increased their chances of employment.

"I don't see myself as an American," Erna said.

Vache didn't see himself as an American either. That country was too right-wing for his left-leaning views. "Britain might be better."

Erna frowned. "It might be," she eventually said. "But only if they accept our qualifications."

Which may not happen. Vache put his phone down, sat up in bed and kissed his beautiful, dark-haired wife. "Come my love," he said. "Let's have breakfast."

"And the future?"

"That depends on our qualifications, and next week we'll have to check on that. Otherwise, Jordan or Lebanon."

Erna slid out of bed, and went to the living room as she was. Vache was surprised. She looked over her shoulder.

"Don't you think it's delightfully decadent to make love in the morning, and then have breakfast together?"

Vache went to Erna where she touched his muscular chest. He admired her slim and feminine body, and she was right. That was delightfully decadent!

* * *

It was a mild, September evening, and getting dark early as autumn moved towards winter. As always on a Monday, Ranim waited at al-Rasheed Park, and as always she stood when Adnan approached, and as always he kissed her soft cheek. Today she wore simple light green dress half-way to her knees, and a dark green hijab. Adnan took her small hand and they strolled into the park, illuminated by lights from adjacent streets. Past the statue surrounded by seats, all vacant, and along the path to trees beyond.

"It's very quiet," Ranim said.

"They're all at home watching bad news on the television," Adnan said flatly.

"I'm tired of bad news on the television."

"Let's forget about that tonight," Adnan said. "Tonight it's just us."

"Yes it is," Ranim said softly; her voice barely carrying above the noise of traffic beyond.

Deeper into the trees, and it was hard to imagine they were in the centre of a city of 220,000 people. In that tree garden, it was as if they were alone in the world. On either side of the path were seats, where Adnan guided Ranim to sit.

He put his arm around her shoulder and she rested her head against his shoulder.

"We're all alone," she said quietly; in a repeat of Adnan's thoughts.

Adnan's heart beat fast, and his hands were sweaty despite the cool. He squeezed Ranim tighter and felt her relax against him. He turned his head and kissed her lips, and touched those lips with his tongue. Soft, warm, moist. He kissed her while luxuriating in that moistness, and momentarily fantasising about other things. He squeezed her shoulders tighter and kissed more passionately too; until she pulled away.

"Somebody will see us," Ranim said.

"There's nobody around," Adnan said.

She looked up and he knew she saw nobody, and he held her face and kissed her again, and this time her tongue met his. Adnan gripped Ranim's shoulders, soft through the thin cotton of her dress. He stroked her soft arms, and felt the straps of her bra under. He fantasised about her bra, her breasts, more. There, now.

His kissing became more and more urgent, and his hands wandered to her legs; smooth and firm through thin cotton. Along her legs, lower and lower, until he touched soft skin. Slowly and slowly he bunched her dress, touching her smooth, soft thighs. Smooth, soft, all woman.

"I want you," Adnan murmured.

"We can't."

He touched her lips with his tongue again, and her mouth opened to invite him in. Again their tongues touched while Adnan stroked her soft thighs. His heart beat fast and he felt short of breath, until he remembered to breathe. Tongues flicked and flicked again, and Adnan sensed she wanted him as much as he wanted her. Until she pulled her head away and he took his hand from her legs. She looked down at the paving all around.

"I love you but we can't," she said. "Not yet."

Adnan took her chin and looked into her eyes. He knew what to say. "I love you Ranim, and because I love you this is all we'll do."

"For now."

Adnan understood, except there were too many obstacles in their way. He stood and took Ranim's hand. She walked beside him in silence, all the way to her home.

* * *

Adnan had a restless night. They loved each other, they matched each other in all ways; in fact he couldn't imagine a more wonderful woman in all of Raqqah. In all of Syria. In the entire world. If he asked to marry Ranim, he knew she would say 'yes', if only that were possible. Adnan was far away at work that day, until he decided to visit Ranim's family that evening. Perhaps Ranim had had a solution for their problem.

Adnan climbed concrete steps two at a time to the third floor, and knocked on their door. He greeted Ustaaz Fakhri and was invited in. They discussed the weather for a moment, before Adnan asked if he could take Ranim out for a walk. Of course he could, and a short while later they were on the street. But Adnan didn't know where to start.

"I just want to say...," Ranim said, and Adnan turned his head to look at her. "I just want to say that I love you." She took his hand. "I love you and I know you love me."

"What do you think we should do?" he asked.

"You should ask me to marry you, but my father wants me to finish school."

"When's that?"

"In June next year."

That wasn't so long, but they still had the problem of money. And then the answer came. "I'll ask my father for wages to support a wife, and if he can't do that, then I'll find a job which can."

"Of course!" Ranim exclaimed. "Your father can't deny you marriage and children. When we marry I can work in a shop or something like that, and that way we can get started."

Adnan was surprised their solution came so easily.

"These days, couples don't have children straight away," Ranim said. "I'll find out how that happens, so I can work until we establish ourselves."

Adnan stopped, took both of her hands and looked into her eyes. "I'm glad this is happening," he said, and he really was.

"I am too. Now you can ask me."

"Ranim my love; will you marry me?"

She kissed his lips. "Yes my love; I will marry you. Now you have to ask my father."

That was right. They could get engaged now for marriage next year. There was one other thing, but Adnan felt embarrassed. "When you find about not having children," Adnan said while feeling hot and flushed, and looking at her sandals. "Can you find about not having children now?"

Ranim smiled brightly, and Adnan sensed she knew what he meant. "Yes, I will. But first, you must do your duty."

Adnan looked into her eyes again. "Ustaaz Fakhri," he said. "I would like to marry your wonderful daughter Ranim, next year after she finishes school."

Ranim smiled brightly, and led Adnan towards her family's apartment.

* * *

Adnan unlocked the door of their apartment and let himself inside. Mama came from the kitchen and her expression changed.

"What's wrong?" she asked.

31

"Nothing's wrong," Adnan said. "I asked Ranim to marry me and Ustaaz Fakhri agreed."

Mama hugged him tight. "That's good news Adnan. Ranim's a lovely girl and I'm sure she'll make a wonderful wife."

"You're marrying Ranim?" Lina asked.

"Yes I am," Adnan said.

Mama moved away to let Lina hug Adnan. "Ranim's wonderful and I'm sure you'll be happy together. I often see her with her friends, and that's always a good sign. When you see four inseparable friends you know they all have good hearts."

"We're marrying in June next year."

"After she finishes year twelve?"

"Yes."

"What's this about marriage?" Papa asked.

"Adnan's marrying Ranim in June next year," Mama said.

"That's good news Adnan. She comes from a good family."

"That's not important!" Mama exclaimed. "Ranim's a wonderful girl; you can see that. Whenever she's been here it seems like she belongs with us, and I just know they'll be happy together. I feel like I'm gaining a daughter rather than losing a son."

"And I'm gaining an older sister!" Lina exclaimed.

Adnan was quite surprised that his family thought so highly of Ranim; but then he thought he shouldn't be surprised. She was good and kind and considerate and capable and confident and smart, and especially beautiful!

"What are you thinking about?" Lina asked.

"My fiancee," Adnan said while smiling brightly.

"Now we must cook a special meal for this good news evening," Mama said. "Lina; can you help me?"

They left for the kitchen, to leave Adnan and Papa in the living room. "Now you need a pay rise," Papa said. "Living at home you don't need to earn so much, but now that you're getting married you need proper wages."

"Only if you can afford it," Adnan said; not wanting to hurt the family's finances.

"Of course I can! You're very capable at work; so capable that business has never been better." He patted Adnan on his back. "I'm proud of you my son. You passed year twelve at school, and that education will help you to cope with future challenges in life. A good women like Ranim will only fall in love with a good man like you." Papa hugged him. "I'm proud of everything you've done, and I'm certain you'll be happy with Ranim. She's a bright girl and she'll be a good life's partner."

Adnan hugged his Papa. "Thank you Papa," he said quietly, while sensing Mama looking from the doorway. Adnan was truly surprised. They knew Ranim of course, and she'd had lunch with the family a few times too, and clearly she'd made a good impression. Papa was right; beyond everything else Ranim was bright.

"Dinner's ready," Mama said, and Adnan looked to see Mama still smiling brightly.

"Papa's right," she said. "Good women only fall in love with good men like you." Mama hugged Adnan and he felt her love in that embrace, although he often felt his parents' love, and Lina's love too. He came from the most loving family in Raqqah. Adnan stood back and admired his Papa and Mama; ordinary Syrians but at the same time very special. His family who loved him so much.

Chapter Four

Vache watched protestors gathering one year and one day after the first calls to oust Assad. Friday March 16, 2012, and there'd been protests every Friday for many months, and a mounting death toll as the government turned on its own, even though they protested peacefully with banners, flags and slogans. According to independent news reports, about 30 to 40 unarmed protestors were killed each week. In addition, the Free Syrian Army battled the government army in suburbs of larger cities, including Damascus and especially in Homs. The United Nations and even the father-in-law of Bashar al-Assad condemned this government-wrought violence, but to no avail. Officers and soldiers continued to defect to the Free Syrian Army, or defected out of the battle and into Turkey. That was understandable when the orders were to kill your own.

State television reported terrorists, while international news websites, freely available, presented a more balanced view of the many anti-government protests, a small number of pro-government demonstrations, and continuing killings of Syrian civilians by the Syrian Army. Social media and discussion forums played their part in keeping regular Friday protests rolling across the country. The Syrian civil unrest was like none before. It was unrest mobilised through internet cafes and wi-fi networks.

Vache stayed indoors and watched the day unfold on his laptop. A massive protest, equal in scale to April the previous year, gathered in the city centre. But this time there was a significant army presence, although reports were that some of that army had defected to the Free Syrian Army. Many Syrians used their smartphones to record the army firing live rounds into an unarmed crowd, and what seemed like battles between two different armies. The battles of Damascus and Homs had come to the most boring city in Syria. Eventually protestors dispersed, to leave paramedics with ambulances to pick up the pieces.

"Do you think this is the time to go?" Erna asked.

Vache didn't want to make that decision on his own. "What do you think?"

Erna frowned. "We're not in danger," she eventually said. "The killing of protestors is wrong, but if we don't protest then we're not in danger."

"Then we stay?" Vache asked.

"Yes, we can stay for now."

* * *

Adnan waited in his rented suit, and pulled at the collar tight at his neck. The men of the groom's party waited alongside dressed in their best. Noise on the staircase and Ranim appeared dressed in white with a bouquet in her hands, and looking stunning in the dress she made with her mother. The crowd clapped and cheered enthusiastically, while local musicians played; especially loud drums. Ranim, accompanied by her father, climbed the stairs to Adnan's family's apartment, and then took Adnan's hand to be escorted inside.

There the imam waited, and in a stern voice he told Adnan how Prophet Muhammad, peace be upon him, honoured his wives, and Adnan must honour his wife in the same way. Then the imam told Ranim that she must honour her husband, and treat him well and with respect. Adnan agreed with what had been spoken, and Ustaaz Fakhri then agreed with the proposal. Ranim and Adnan placed rings on each other's right hand. With that the documents, waiting on a table, were signed and witnessed, and Adnan and Ranim were married.

The couple were escorted to the hall accompanied by music, cheering and impromptu dancing. The wedding guests were dressed in their best, and they looked superb for a big celebration in the neighbourhood. The wedding party reached the hall, decorated inside and out with banners and bunting. To music and cheering, Ranim escorted by Adnan, danced her way into the hall. Seven men, led by Hardi as lawweeh, performed the dabke; all dancing and stomping to the beat of the music; especially loud drums. Adnan escorted Ranim to their table, where the music and dancing stopped but not the noise of celebration. Holding a knife hand over hand they cut the multi-layered cake, and then exchanged their rings from right hands to left hands, before Ranim threw her bouquet over her head to single women waiting behind to catch. The woman who caught the bouquet would be the next to marry. With that Adnan could dance with his beautiful wife, followed by all guests dancing, and that was boisterous and exuberant.

The dancing went long into the afternoon, after which waiting food was uncovered, and the women of the neighbourhood had put much effort into preparing a lavish feast. While he ate, Adnan stepped aside so he could admire his wife in white, smiling brightly. It was obvious she was bursting with happiness, and Adnan was so pleased to be married to such a bright woman. Momentarily he remembered where they started, with a chance meeting at school. There he spoke to a girl a few years younger, attracted by her looks to be sure, but more attracted by her maturity. He was in his final year while Ranim was two years younger, and when their paths crossed again he invited her out. From then they were a couple, and destined to marry. Today they were married, with a hundred guests or more celebrating their special day.

After a long and happy celebration, it was time to head to a new home; three streets away in the same neighbourhood. Ranim helped find their small apartment in an older-style building, and together they chose bedding, curtains and other furnishings. They climbed the stairs to the first floor where Adnan unlocked the door. He stood aside to let Ranim enter, and locked the door behind. Ranim removed her veil and laid it on the bed before she kissed Adnan.

'I love you," she said quietly.

"I love you too," he replied.

Adnan stepped back. Ranim's dress was skin tight and highlighted her feminine curves, and for the past hours he'd fantasised about what lay beneath although he already knew. He smiled at those memories.

"What's so funny?" she asked.

"We've been here before, more than once," he said.

She smiled brightly. "Yes we have. Now unclip my dress, and we can make love as husband and wife for the first time."

With his hands shaking slightly, Adnan unclipped the back of her dress, and eased the zip downwards. He watched as Ranim wriggled her dress over her hips, revealing her white, lacy bra. He watched her remove that, and her white, lacy panties too. She came to him in white stockings and shoes, and hugged him to kiss. He kissed while cupping her firm, fleshy bottom in his hands.

* * *

On a cloudy, autumn day, Sarya trudged home after a long day at school. Each year meant harder work, and now early in year ten, her classes were hardest yet. She was glad to

reach home where she kicked off her shoes and went inside
to the living room: the largest room in the house: painted
green; with green and white ceramic tiles, a green carpet, and
green cushions along two walls. There was a glass-fronted
timber cabinet with family heirlooms on display, and a
television on a stand. Sarya greeted her mother in the kitchen
just beyond, before going to her room on the other side of
the hallway. That room was pale pink, and had a dark pink
mattress on the floor with red cushions around, and with the
quilt rolled up. There was a chest for her clothes, which
Sarya kept neatly folded. Also off that hallway was the
bedroom for her parents, and an empty bedroom where
Daran once slept.

From her chest Sarya grabbed her smartphone, and sat
against cushions to read about that day's momentous events.
Assad's forces had just withdrawn from the regions of Afrin,
Jazira and Kobanî; handing large parts of northern Syria to
the Kurdish People's Protection Units. Just like that; the
Kurdish people of Syria had autonomy. When Sarya
protested over a year before, she never would have believed
that outcome.

In the rest of Syria, war raged. She read that the
Islamic State of Iraq and the Levant, which had joined Jabhat
al-Nusra as the main Islamic opposition players, wanted to
restore the caliphate of early Islam. What started as a
revolution for democracy had turned into the Islamisation of

Syria. Sarya frowned while she read that, because it didn't make sense to her. That was very complicated, whatever it was.

Mama called to help prepare dinner, and they had just finished when Papa came home from school. Being headmaster, he worked a longer day. Sarya greeted him, he greeted her, and then he looked at her.

"You have something on your mind," Papa said.

"I do," Sarya said. "Our People's Protection Units now have taken control of our land which is good. Then I read about the Islamic State of Iraq and the Levant wanting to restore the caliphate of early Islam, but I don't know what that means."

Papa frowned while he thought. "I don't know what that means either. It could be important though."

"How?"

"Well, if the Islamic State of Iraq and the Levant defeat Assad's depleted forces, they may threaten us."

"I can look up caliphate on my smartphone," Sarya said.

"You could, but a clearer understanding might come from speaking with someone who knows. You should speak with the imam at the mosque, and he would know."

That was true. "I'll speak with the imam tomorrow, after school," Sarya said.

"When you find out you can tell us."

41

"I will."

The next day Sarya went to the women's entrance of the mosque, removed her shoes, washed her hands and face, and went inside. But that didn't help because the imam was in the men's section. There were no prayers at that time, so Sarya thought it would be alright. She went through the other door where a man in white arranged prayer mats.

"Excuse me," Sarya said in Arabic a quiet voice.

The imam stood up straight.

"My name's Sarya Goran, and I would like to ask you a question."

"Marhaba Sarya," he said.

"Marhaba," Sarya replied. "I read about the Islamic State of Iraq and the Levant wanting to restore the caliphate of early Islam, but I don't know what that means. Can you tell me please?"

"Of course Sarya. A caliphate is an area containing an Islamic steward known as a caliph, who's considered the religious successor to Prophet Muhammad, peace be upon him, and the leader of the entire Muslim community. The caliphate of early Islam, is Islam as it was in the Seventh Century."

Sarya frowned while she digested that. "As Muslims, that would make Islamic State in charge of you and me," she said.

"That would, and that's controversial. Also, Islam of the Seventh Century is very different to Islam of today. Many freedoms you have as a woman would be denied to you, such as going to school, the clothes you wear today, and even coming here on your own."

Sarya didn't like that at all. She had the freedom to be whoever she wanted to be, and she didn't want to go back to even Mama's time, let alone more than a thousand years ago. "Do you have an opinion on this?"

"I believe such a move would be unacceptable to many in our community."

Sarya understood. "Thank you," she said. "Marhaba."

"Marhaba."

Sarya left the men's areas, put on her shoes, and headed home. She couldn't wait until Papa came home so she could tell him. As always Papa had been right. She doubted she could have found that on the internet, and even if she did, she doubted she would have understood it. Papa was a clever man.

They discussed Sarya's findings after eating, where Papa was clear in his views. He believed there had to be a separation between religion and government, and restoring an ancient caliphate would destroy that separation. Sarya understood and she agreed with him, although Mama seemed confused by it all.

Autumn meant cooler weather and even rain, where normally dry, dusty streets turned to mud and slush. Sarya walked home protected by her parka with a hood; with her books safe in her backpack, while cars swished by trailing spray. She was pleased to reach home where she could catch up on the battles between the People's Protection Units: the YPG[1] and the YPJ[2], with Jabhat al-Nusra l'Ahl as-Sham at Ras al-Ayn. Syrian internet stopped long ago, but mobile data from Turkey was cheaply available. Sarya read about those battles before going to the Facebook page of Lions of Rojava. There she read the latest posts about brave men and women fighting for Kurdish freedom. There were many pictures and film clips, and some of those women of the YPJ could have been her. Sarya lay on her back and wondered. Should she be safe at home when girls her age risked their lives for her freedom? Sarya thought not. She was 16 years and three months old, and she could volunteer. But her parents! Sarya wondered how she could convince them, or should she just run away and let them know when she was gone? Sarya was sure some girls her age did that! But she didn't want to hurt her parents that way. Somehow she had to discuss this with Mama and Papa.

---

[1] YPG - Yekineyen Parastina Gel or Peoples Protection Units
[2] YPJ - Yekineyen Parastina Jin or Women's Protection Units

Sarya still wondered about how she could talk about joining the YPJ when she heard her father's voice. They were eating kofta, kartolên pîvazan, with tea.

"Sarya; you're sharing our meal but you're not in this room," Papa said.

"Sorry," Sarya said, feeling flushed despite the cool. "It's just I read about the battles with Jabhat al-Nusra and...."

"And?" Papa asked.

Sarya looked down at the food on the cloth. "And, well, I wondered if I should be safe when others risk their lives for our freedom?"

Sarya looked up at Papa who smiled brightly. "Do you want to join the YPJ?" he asked.

Sarya nodded.

"War isn't like what you see on pictures and videos," he said.

"I don't know what war is," Sarya said. "But I do know how I feel."

"I understand," Papa said.

"I don't understand," Mama said. "Why do you want to go to war?"

"Because we've fought invaders for thousands of years," Sarya said automatically.

"This is true," Papa said, while Mama frowned.

"Women haven't fought invaders," Mama said firmly.

"This is a new time," Papa said.

45

"You just want to send my daughter to war."

"Where do we draw the line? How can Sarya have a career like a man, and not take on responsibility for our safety?"

"But she's too young!"

Sarya felt uncomfortable while her parents argued. She wished she'd never raised the issue.

"I would like Sarya to finish school first," Papa said.

Sarya was disappointed by that.

"At sixteen you're too young, although I know some girls do," Papa said. "At eighteen you'll be mature enough to handle yourself in war, and you'll have an education to fall back on when this is over."

"You'll let me volunteer when I finish school?" Sarya clarified, in case she misunderstood.

"Now you must ask Mama."

Sarya looked to Mama, who took a deep breath before taking Sarya's hands and looking into her eyes. "Your Papa's right when he said this is a new time for women, and Papa's also right when he said you should finish school first, because education will give you opportunities that I didn't have. So finish school, and you'll have my blessings to go to war. But please be careful my darling."

Sarya grabbed Mama and hugged her, and felt her eyes go moist. She really loved her parents, and she knew they loved her. They loved her enough to let her join the YPJ, and no parent's love was stronger than that.

Chapter Five

The airstrikes on opposition forces were relentless. To Vache it seemed incongruous to be in the relative luxury of an air-conditioned apartment on a fine, early-March day, while just a few kilometres away, Syrian Air Force jets pounded the forces of the Free Syrian Army, Jabhat al-Nusra, and the Islamic State of Iraq and the Levant, which had joined the conflict some months previously. The speed of the opposition advance on Raqqah was indicative of a dispirited army, or what was left of a dispirited army after many defections.

Erna paced the room while Vache admired her lovely figure in jeans and a white t-shirt. When you're beautiful with a light-olive complexion, dark eyes, shoulder-length, black hair, slim and medium-busted; then jeans and a t-shirt was all that was needed. However, their future was uncertain once that the Islamic State of Iraq and the Levant, known as DAESH in Arabic, joined the fight against Assad. In the view of DAESH, Christians were unwelcome while women were unworthy, and a woman in jeans and a t-shirt was tantamount to damnation in hell.

"You should sit," Vache said.

Erna sat opposite him on the blue, cloth-covered corner couch that made up the main furnishing of their living room.

"What were you thinking about?" Vache said.

"What I discovered about DAESH in Iraq," Erna replied. "We now know that DAESH are reproducing what they believe to be the purest form of Islam, which is Islam as it was in the Seventh Century, including major repression of women. They've recruited extremist fighters through the internet, by the notion that DAESH are the true custodians of Islamic belief, even though the vast majority of Muslims have a liberal interpretation of their religion. More worryingly, DAESH aim to conquer all who do not believe in their interpretation of the Quran, which includes most Muslims and all other religions."

"DAESH also promise their fighters money, power and sex. Money through oil revenue, power over a subjugated population, and sex through non-Islamic women captured as sex slaves. That puts you at risk."

"We must get out of Raqqah."

"We can't leave through the middle of a pitched battle, so we have to wait until opposition forces win. Then we can go."

"Any ideas?"

"Out of Syria and across the border to Sanliurfa in Turkey. From there we can arrange our next move to Jordan or Lebanon; probably Amman in Jordan."

"What about returning to Aleppo?"

"The war in Aleppo is worse than here, and our families should leave Aleppo if they can."

"I'm Christian so we must keep a distance from DAESH when we go."

That was true; that was very true, but the answer to that problem would come in time.

It took just two days for combined opposition forces to seize most of Raqqah, with the strange sight of Free Syrian Army tanks rumbling along streets normally swarming with traffic. The remnants of the Syrian Army made a last stand in the city centre, but defeat was inevitable given they were vastly outnumbered. After a third day of battle, the 6th of March 2013, the city of Raqqah was in the control of opposition forces. International news websites reported executions of Syrian Army commanders at Naeem Roundabout, while from his window; the sight of armed DAESH militants in black was unsettling. The majority of the population didn't think so, and many Arabs noisily celebrated the liberation of Raqqah from the brutal and corrupt Assad regime. They were genuinely jubilant, although Vache suspected they didn't know the true nature of one of the forces which liberated their city.

The dark, cool, grocery shop was from a bygone era of fruit and vegetables on wooden benches, and milk and other drinks in a glass-fronted refrigerator; eternally rumbling.

"Marhaba Doctor Vache," Anas, the grocer, greeted.

"Marhaba Anas," Vache replied.

"Can I get you something?"

Vache glanced around the shop and saw nobody. "Erna and I think we should leave Raqqah, but not in full view."

"It's a pity you have to leave."

"We're young and we can start over, and we can return when things settle down."

"Aren't you pleased that Raqqah has been liberated?"

"In some ways I'm pleased, but we're uncertain about the future for Christians."

"For me and for most in Raqqah, we know that we're the same, except we worship God in different ways."

"I'm only being careful, and one day we can come back."

"It's important to be careful at this time of war."

"I would prefer not to go by bus," Vache said.

Anas scratched his balding head. "I have suppliers who come from the countryside, and I know someone who can take you in his truck."

That would be ideal. "Either they can take us through opposition forces beyond the city, and we can catch a bus from there, or they can take us to Turkey."

"Turkey would be safe for you, I think."

Vache thought that was ironic, given Turks had driven Armenians out of their now country, and killed a million and a half in a barbaric atrocity. But that was long ago, and two

Armenians would be safe in Turkey while they arranged their next move.

"You leave this with me, Doctor Vache," Anas said. "I'll let you know."

Later that afternoon, Hafeez, the youngest son of Anas, told Vache in his recently broken voice, to be at the shop at five the next morning.

It was strange to lock the door on their apartment; leaving all but which could be carried in backpacks each. Hopefully they would return in the not too distant future and pick up where they left off.

In early dawn light, Abdul worked at unloading vegetables in the narrow lane to the rear of the shop. He was about forty, a bit pudgy, and dressed in grey trousers and a red, chequered, flannelette shirt. They greeted each other in turn and all shook hands, after which the offer was one-hundred pounds to the city outskirts, or three-hundred pounds to Sanliurfa. Vache agreed to pay three-hundred pounds, before he and Erna climbed into the back of an old and somewhat battered, olive green Bedford truck. The tray of the truck had a canvas hood stretched over a steel frame, and held empty wooden crates probably from the previous week's delivery. Vache helped Erna to pick her way over those crates to hide at the forward end of the cargo area; protected from view.

The engine roared and they jerked into motion on a still, spring morning. Abdul wasted no time in getting to what seemed a fairly outrageous speed, while Vache struggled to brace himself while they hurtled around corners. On and on until brakes squealed sharply, and they were thrown forward as the truck shuddered to a halt. Loud voices approached, and they'd driven into the midst of opposition fighters! The driver's door squeaked while Vache heard Abdul say that he was returning home after a delivery, but nervously and hesitantly. Another voice asked if there was anything in the rear, to which Abdul replied there were empty crates, but again nervously and suspiciously.

Footsteps crunched on gravel while Vache signalled Erna to get low, and ducked as low as he could get himself. The tailgate fell open with a crash; then crates were pulled out and noisily tossed to the ground. Vache looked around but there was nothing but those crates to hide behind, so he backed to the far corner where he felt rough and coarse material. Hessian for sure, so he threw a bag over Erna and climbed under hessian himself.

Soldiers pulled crates out one by one, while Vache was sure he and Erna would be caught. If those soldiers were DAESH they would take Erna as a sex slave. Vache snuggled lower, and hoped that in the early, dawn light, they wouldn't be spotted. It was critical they weren't spotted. The last crates were roughly unloaded leaving Vache, Erna and their backpacks covered by hessian bags. Somebody climbed on board and walked along the cargo tray in heavy footsteps. Closer and closer until he kicked at the hessian, and Vache bit his lip to stifle a grunt at the sharp pain. Footsteps moved away while Abdul babbled about carrying nothing but empty crates. A voice told Abdul to load his truck and get out of there, which Abdul quickly did. After a few minutes they were on their way once more. After a while the truck squealed to a stop, and Vache wondered 'what now?'.

"You can come out now, Doctor Vache," Abdul said while he dropped the tailgate.

Vache struggled to his feet bent over, and gave his hand to Erna who also stood bent over. Carefully they picked their way over empty crates and jumped to the ground.

"Soldiers stopped us back there," Abdul said. "There's nobody around now, so we're safe."

Vache gazed across the bleak and featureless plain which made up much of northern Syria. It stretched as far as he could see, with not a building or even a tree to break the monotony. Actually there were villages every ten or so kilometres, where ancient mud-brick houses had been replaced by more substantial structures built in concrete blocks. Apart from more modern houses, farmers lived as they had for centuries.

"You can ride up front," Abdul said.

54

Abdul climbed up, Vache got into the middle of a cracked and faded, green vinyl seat, and Erna sat to the right and banged the door shut.

Into gear and away, and soon they were speeding in a relative sense across that plain.

"It's good for you to leave Raqqah, I think," Abdul said. "I don't like those soldiers in black."

Those in black were DAESH militants. "Do you live in a village?" Vache asked.

"I do."

"You should be safe there."

"Yes, we should be safe."

On and on for about an hour, until they reached the border at Akçakale, where passports were stamped and the Turkish border guard wearily waved the truck away. Away once more; speeding through villages every so often, until they reached Sanliurfa after another hour's driving. It was still early while they navigated the big city of more than half a million. A modern city with much development taking place over recent decades. Closing on the centre, where Vache asked Abdul to find them a hotel. Abdul screeched to a stop at the Hilton Garden Inn, where the doorman helped Erna from the old and battered truck. Abdul went to the back and retrieved their backpacks. Vache thanked Abdul with genuine sincerity, and gave him five-hundred pounds because he'd earned that. He watched Abdul climb into his no doubt precious truck, and speed away in a cloud of fumes.

Vache followed the doorman into a bland, brightly lit foyer finished in sandy-coloured granite, with indoor plants dotted here and there. At reception Vache booked a room which was available, so they went to the fifth floor and unpacked their bags.

"Now what?" Erna said.

"We can use hotel wi-fi to find the hospital in Amman," Vache said. "We can ring their personnel department and see if we can get a job there, or get their help to find a job somewhere else." He looked at his watch and it was almost eight. "It's too early for that now. We should explore the old city," he said. He was curious about old Urfa.

Vache wandered through the inner city of Sanliurfa: an ancient labyrinth of narrow streets and lanes crowded by three and four-storey, stone buildings. It had barely changed for centuries, except for cars lining wider streets, and ugly power lines tacked onto buildings. Other than that, inner Sanliurfa, once known as Urfa or Ourfa to Armenians, was the same as when his ancestors once lived there, about a century before.

He reached the largest building in the old city and stopped, transfixed by the Selahettin Eyyubi Mosque, once the Armenian Apostolic Cathedral of the Holy Mother of God. The scene of the last stand by Armenians before they

56

were deported. He tried to picture what that would have been like, but couldn't.

"This hasn't always been a mosque," Erna said.

"It was an Armenian Apostolic Cathedral," Vache said. "In Urfa they knew about the genocide, so they decided to stand and fight. A few thousand men and a number of women kept the Ottoman Army at bay for a few months, before they were defeated and the inevitable happened. Surviving men were killed, while women and children were taken on a death march to Aleppo. One of those women fighters was Anoush Hagopian. She survived along with her oldest daughter Karine and her son Taniel. Karine and her husband Paul Lang later adopted two refugee children."

"Ah, this makes sense. They're your relatives."

"Come with me," Vache said.

The Hilton Garden Inn was only a ten minute walk away, and soon they were inside bland modernity once more, complete with climate control and double glazing. Vache went to his backpack, and from the bottom he retrieved an ancient, hard-covered scrapbook. He sat on the bed and Erna sat beside him. He turned the pages to show photos protected by clear, plastic leaves.

"Paul Lang was a Swiss doctor," Vache said. "He came to Aleppo to gather evidence about the genocide, where he found Karine Hagopian in a brothel, having been sold into sex slavery. He bought Karine from that brothel and she helped him to take these pictures. Later they found and rescued Anoush and Taniel. Karine, Paul and Anoush spent the next few years raising money, before returning to Aleppo after the war to rescue women who'd been kidnapped or sold."

Vache turned the page to a yellowing newspaper article written in French. A picture of man and a woman on horses; the man staring into the distance and the woman looking down at the camera. "This is Karine and Paul," he said.

Erna lightly brushed the plastic film. "She was beautiful," she gasped. "What she saw; what she experienced. And yet she came back with her husband to help other survivors. He must have loved her to devote his life to the Armenian cause."

Vache thought that was more than just love.

"Look at her clothes," Erna said. "A long dress clinched at the waist by a belt, and riding up because she's astride a horse to reveal tough, lace-up boots. And her headscarf. Amazing. Islam merely copied what was a long-standing cultural practice in this part of the world."

That was true. "Karine was known for her black and white views," Vache said. "There were no shades of grey. It was good or it was bad; it was right or it was wrong, and if it was right then you put your heart and soul into it."

"There's a lesson there. DAESH is wrong; the most wrong since the genocide of a hundred years ago. We have to put our hearts and souls into destroying DAESH."

Vache agreed. "There's no obvious way to do that now, but one day a path will reveal itself, and when it does we must follow it."

"You said they adopted children."

"Two refugee Armenian children from the Turkish War of Independence. Given Karine was sold to a brothel, I would guess she was infertile from Chlamydia."

Erna touched the plastic again. "What I would do to change places with Karine Hagopian for just one day, to know what she saw and what she went through." Erna looked at Vache. "Now we know what we must do."

When the path revealed itself, they would follow it.

* * *

Adnan bought an hour's time at the internet cafe and logged on using the code on a scrap of paper. First he went to al-Jazeera and read the day's news, and it was good news about Raqqah. Proudly, the first city liberated from Assad was recovering from the past year, with schools and universities open once more, and provincial councils formed to manage neighbourhoods. From time to time there were airstrikes from that brute Assad, but despite that Raqqah had a feeling of peace and calm.

Adnan then went to Facebook, and paused while he thought about the marvels of being friends with Arabs in other parts of Syria, and friends with Arabs across the world; connected through the internet by a common heritage and a common language. From his News Feed, Adnan scanned what his friends were up to. He was surprised to see Ammar concerned about the Islamic State of Iraq and the Levant. Adnan read the posting about Islamic State's accusations of traitors within the Free Syrian Army, and accusations of traitors within Jabhat al-Nusra, with weapons being stolen from both. Adnan wondered if there was truth in that posting because it didn't make sense for opposition forces to fight amongst themselves. He posted that comment before logging off and heading home.

They had a 90 square metre, two bedroom apartment all painted in beige, with grey vinyl flooring. The living area was to the right of the entrance, complete with a laminate table and four laminate chairs, a sofa against the wall, and the television on a stand. Off that room was a narrow kitchen with patterned grey wallpaper to shoulder high, and this had darker beige painted cupboards, a sink, a stove, and the refrigerator they bought. The kitchen led to the small bathroom finished in grey tiles, which had a bath with shower over, a sink, a toilet, and the shaving cupboard with a mirror. To the left of the entrance was a corridor with two bedrooms; one unused. Their bedroom had a queen-sized bed and their wardrobe, with hanging space above and drawers below, with both finished in varnished pine.

Ranim emerged from the kitchen. "You've been at the internet cafe," she said with a big smile.

"This is a historic time, and I can keep in touch with that through the internet," Adnan replied. He paused while he considered the marvel of it. "I couldn't imagine not being connected to the rest of the world through the internet."

"We should be connected anytime we like," Ranim said. "We can afford that now, and you can get rid of your old monstrosity of a mobile!"

That was true given Ranim recently received a pay increase at the pharmacy, where she served behind the counter. "Tomorrow we'll get smartphones."

"You get yours and I'll buy one for me."

Ranim liked to be independent, and had proven to be very practical with their money. She budgeted their spending on rent, food, electricity, gas and other essentials, and saved a fair amount on top of that.

"Now my love, I shall cook dinner."

Adnan thought that Ranim worked hard at her job and deserved an evening off. "Let's go out," he said.

A big smile showed agreement. Soon after, they wandered through the market where many vendors were cooking at stalls. They feasted on felafil, shawarma or meat in bread, and kanafeh or pastry with sweet cheese and nuts.

A little further on was a phone vendor, and shortly after they had Samsung Galaxy SIIs each, a previous model and cheaper, on plans with Syriatel.

Back at the apartment Adnan set up an account with the Google Play store and downloaded Facebook, al-Jazeera and scanned for other apps. Twitter and he downloaded that as well. Weather, and he found a well-reviewed app and downloaded that also.

"If I knew you were going to spend all night on that phone, I wouldn't have suggested buying it!" Ranim said as she emerged from their bedroom.

"I'll only be a moment," Adnan said, while he wondered what other apps would be useful.

"Are you coming to bed my love?" Ranim asked from the bedroom doorway.

"I'll only be a minute."

Adnan sensed something and looked up to see Ranim stark naked in front of him with her hands on her hips. He was momentarily shocked, and then aroused. Fair complexion; small, slim and yet busty, her broad hips and what lay between, discreet and hairless. He put his phone down and followed Ranim to their bedroom, where over the past months he'd discovered that the traditional teaching was true. When God created desire He made it into ten parts, and He gave nine of those parts to women. No matter where he touched Ranim she responded passionately: from her lips to the lobes of her ears, her breasts and nipples, the flat of her stomach, the inside of her smooth thighs, and especially between her legs. Each part of her responded a different touch, lighter or firmer, but with the right touch she could experience pleasure over and over again. That part of making love was more exciting than intercourse, as good as that was. And yet intercourse, the delight of being connected body to body, was the ultimate pleasure too. For sure, man was only half when he didn't have the love of a woman.

Chapter Six

Gunfire on the cold streets of Raqqah. January 2014, and the streets were damp and slushy when tensions between Jabhat al-Nusra and the Free Syrian Army towards the Islamic State of Iraq and the Levant, boiled over into battles on the streets. That had been building over the past few months, and especially when Islamic State seized from the ranks of other armies, those who they called traitors, who were then executed. Business at the cafe fell away, while Adnan kept in touch with what was happening through al-Jazeera and through his Facebook friends. Small battles raged with gunshots echoing through streets, which quickly emptied when skirmishes broke out. From the safety of their apartment, Adnan was able to monitor the situation which didn't take long to resolve. Soon the Black Standard, one of the flags of Prophet Muhammad, peace be upon him, and the flag used Abu Muslim when he set into motion the Abbasid caliphate, flew above government buildings. DAESH soldiers in black patrolled streets, armed with automatic rifles.

Adnan stopped at the grocers to buy milk on the way home. He went to the fridge and grabbed a plastic bottle before going to the counter.

"Marhaba Anas," Adnan greeted.

"Marhaba Adnan," Anas, the shopkeeper, replied. "Have you heard the news?"

"That the Islamic State of Iraq and the Levant have taken control?"

"Yes there's that, but there's more. They proclaimed we must pray at all set times, and men must attend mosque on Fridays."

Adnan nodded while he thought about that. Of course he believed but he wasn't that devout. He rarely prayed and he rarely attended mosque. "This is a new era for Raqqah," Adnan said as an empty comment, before paying for his milk and heading home. Up the stairs and into their apartment, where he kissed Ranim before putting the milk into their refrigerator.

"Are you alright?" Ranim asked.

"I'm fine," Adnan said. "No. We're expected to pray five times a day, and attend mosque on Friday."

"Will they come into our apartment at dawn, dusk and night to check?"

Adnan was annoyed by that. "This isn't a joking matter!" he snapped. "Prayer is personal, and shouldn't be subject to rules and regulations."

Ranim took his hand and looked into his eyes. "Of course," she said soothingly. "I don't have any respect for these Saudis who've come to Syria to rule us. One part of me thinks we've traded rule by a tyrant for rule by worse tyrants."

Ranim summarised his concerns better than he ever could.

The next day showed the true nature of those tyrants. Customers told Adnan that DAESH held public executions at al-Dallah Roundabout of so-called traitors, including all doctors and nurses from the hospital, because they'd cared for wounded Jabhat al-Nusra and Free Syrian Army soldiers. Those men and women, apparently shot in the head, were no traitors; especially doctors and nurses just doing their jobs. Adnan was shocked that innocent lives could be taken so callously, leaving grieving wives and husbands, and grieving children and families. Ranim and he had bought their furniture and necessary appliances, saved money, and were ready for a family. But the medical facilities of Raqqah had just been destroyed. How could Ranim give birth without a doctor or a nurse? How stupid could DAESH be? Then those victims' bodies were decapitated and their heads impaled on the fence at the roundabout. Every day on his way to work, Adnan walked past those remains of innocent doctors and nurses; left to be picked at by birds and vermin. Adnan tried to pretend they weren't there, because those heads which always stared made him feel sick to his stomach, and because he was scared of what DAESH might do if they saw him looking at what they had done.

Friday really showed what DAESH could do to Adnan, and to any man in Raqqah. The Abdullah bin Masood mosque was packed for prayer, after which the imam read the rules to be followed. The times for prayer were reiterated, women were not allowed out of home unless when absolutely necessary, and when women went outdoors they must be in the company another woman or a male guardian. When out of the home, women must be covered from head to toe, and could only show their eyes. All music but songs without instruments praising jihad, were banned. Men must wear loose fitting pants, with hems falling above their ankles. Smoking was banned, which was tough for those addicted to cigarettes. Hookahs were banned, and alcohol too.

Just outside the mosque was al-Dallah Roundabout, with three young men blindfolded and on their knees. Well aware of DAESH soldiers with rifles all around, Adnan knew Papa and he couldn't turn away. Those men's crimes were read out; no more criminal than doctors and nurses at the hospital, and then a single, sharp shot to the back of the head, each victim slumped forward, dark blood spread, and lives were extinguished. Adnan's heart raced with stress, his stomach heaved, and he was quite stunned that DAESH could even think of behaving so callously; let alone doing what he was just been forced to watch. Adnan sensed many DAESH watching closely, and he feared that even if he turned his head away; he would be their next victim. After the brutality was over; with a heavy heart Adnan returned to Cafe Hamid with Papa. Adnan stayed quiet while he thought about those barbaric executions. He wondered if he would be shot in the back of his head for some trivial misdemeanour. In the future he would have to be very careful of DAESH; be almost invisible to them. Also Adnan pondered the future of his marriage. From that day Ranim was trapped inside a two bedroom apartment, not allowed out unless necessary, for shopping or to visit family, and only if escorted by him or by another woman. And when she went out she had to wear an abaya, a niqab and gloves. Dressed in black from head to foot. His mother too, and his sister Lina, for whom school had just ended. He fell in love with Ranim because she had a good heart, and because she was bright, but surely such an existence would drain her brightness? Surely in repressing women, DAESH were repressing men too? The only connection Ranim would have to the world was through her smartphone, bought at the market when they happily shared food bought from street vendors. Simple pleasures like sharing food from street vendors had just ended, because Ranim couldn't eat in public without revealing her face. What had she done to deserve that?

* * *

Wednesday January 29, 2014, was a historic day for Sarya's people. The three cantons of Rojava: Afrin, Jazira and Kobanî; declared autonomy and adopted the Charter of the Social Contract in Rojava. They discussed that charter in class; paying special attention that all ethnicities and religions in Rojava had equal rights, as did women and children. Two areas stood out: Article 12 stated that Rojava remained an 'integral part of Syria', foreshadowing future federal Syrian governance of the state of Rojava. The other area of interest was direct democracy; known as democratic confederalism. This was participatory democracy with autonomy at the local level; with different local levels such as communes of a number of households, neighbourhoods of a number of communes; then districts of a number of communes and cantons of a number of districts. Delegates at each higher level were elected from the next lowest level: such as communes electing the members of the relevant neighbourhood council, and neighbourhood councils electing members of the relevant district council, and then district councils electing members of the relevant canton council. Beyond that, there were quotas for women at each level. Sarya couldn't take her eyes off her photocopy of the Charter, because she found it fascinating. And then it hit her! Suddenly she realised how brilliant it was.

"You're not with us today, Sarya."

Sarya looked up. "Sorry," she said while she gathered her thoughts. "It's just that our problems have always been race against race and religion against religion. Assad was Shia Arab, and he formed his government out of Shia Arabs which meant Sunni Arabs missed out, and we Kurds were persecuted. But this model is different. Living side-by side, being Arab, Kurd, Shia, Sunni and Christian doesn't matter, as we know. So at the commune level, we'll have all races and religions governing together, because they're used to living together. And then neighbourhoods will be elected from communes, and then districts and finally cantons."

"Well spotted Sarya,"

Sarya was pleased. "This will work well for Rojava" she said, and was convinced it would.

"This model has potential well beyond Rojava. Western democracies have disconnection between what people want, and the priorities of their politicians, who concentrate on accumulating power for themselves. In addition, these power games work against women, who have to play men's games or miss out on democratic participation."

Sarya thought that through. "So that means politics in countries like America and England isn't delivering what it should, and women have difficulties being part of their politics?'

"Our model of democratic confederalism will fix that."

Sarya frowned while she thought about where it started. "This couldn't have happened without our protests," she said.

"Your protests, Sarya."

"Yes, I was part of that, and I was fortunate to be old enough to understand the importance of what we were aiming for then, and I'm old enough to understand the importance of what we've achieved today."

"Indeed we're achieving great things, but now we're running out of time for your next class, so you should discuss these things with your father tonight."

Sarya smiled out of embarrassment. She could never get away from her father being headmaster, and also an advocate for collectivisation and democratic confederalism. Everybody in the city knew her father! Then the bell rang to save Sarya from further embarrassment.

"I'm sure you and your father will have a long discussion tonight," Gulan said with a big smile. "I'm not sure if I should be jealous about that, or relieved that it's not me."

"I think both apply!" Sarya said, and laughed. She was only half-joking. She loved her Papa and she respected the role he played in the community. Change like the Social Contract wouldn't be possible without the local advocacy of people like her Papa, and Sarya enjoyed being a small part of his role in a bigger change. For sure, it was an exciting time to be a Kurdish teenage girl in Rojava.

Chapter Seven

Adnan's smartphone played its alarm tune. He reached across and swiped it off, before wearily rolling out of bed and heading to the bathroom. There he showered before combing his hair, and once more contemplating the beard he had to grow. He dressed in their bedroom; slipping on black tracksuit trousers tucked into longer than normal socks; just like DAESH, and a dark, long-sleeved shirt. In fact that was the only way to dress. In the kitchen, Ranim brewed coffee while the table had dishes of boiled eggs, cheese, mdammas and bread. They shared breakfast in silence, before Adnan kissed her cheek and headed to work.

Downstairs, Raqqah bustled with men and very few women; always in pairs and always enshrouded in black. Those women were out of their homes but still prisoners. Boys headed to school and that was even worse. DAESH used school lessons to brainwash school-age boys into becoming DAESH militants, and even trained those boys to carry out suicide attacks. DAESH insisted all boys go to their schools and parents had no choice in the matter. The only way to prevent that from happening was not to have children, which was a sad choice Adnan and Ranim had to make, until life changed for the better.

Adnan passed the gardens near al-Dallah Roundabout, and as always he tried to ignore many heads impaled on the fence from victims of last Friday's executions. Behind were several rough steel crosses, with victims of crucifixions left to rot in the open while many crows picked at their remains. It was incongruous for women in black to drift through the crowd while holding automatic rifles, but they were the al-Khansa Brigade, to ensure women complied with the DAESH dress code. Even a casually fitted niqab revealing a little face would earn a flogging in the women's prison at the Black Stadium. Al-Hisba men drifted through the crowd too; checking their rules were being adhered to.

Somebody grabbed Adnan by his arm, and Adnan turned to face an al-Hisba who studied Adnan momentarily. Hair long, in fact uncut since January, and a beard, although scrappy. Right clothes, so Adnan knew he was safe.

"A healthy young man like you should join the Islamic State of Iraq and the Levant," the al-Hisba said cheerfully. "We're the true custodians of Islamic belief."

"I would love to join the Islamic State of Iraq and the Levant," Adnan said, even though that was the last thing he would do. He had to be respectful, even though he hated them. "But my father has a business and he relies on me."

The al-Hisba nodded. "Can I see your mobile?" he then asked.

Adnan took his phone from his pocket and handed it across. The al-Hisba checked it over, but Adnan knew what he was looking for from his friends. He'd long turned off his

GPS location, uninstalled Twitter and Facebook, and deleted any music, which would earn a flogging on a Friday, or worse. Adnan watched the al-Hisba frown before he showed Adnan his smartphone.

"Who's this?" the al-Hisba asked.

Adnan's heart skipped a beat, and he felt weak at the knees. The pictures of Ranim naked on their bed; her gift to him. "She's my wife Ranim," Adnan said quietly.

"You treat your wife like a whore."

"She wanted me to take those pictures," Adnan said.

"Which wife would want such a thing?"

"She wanted me to be aroused for her when I come home from work."

"Pictures liked this could earn get you into big trouble."

"I'm sorry for those pictures," he said.

The al-Hisba frowned while Adnan imagined being stripped to the waist outside the mosque that day, and given 40 lashes because of personal pictures of his wife. The pain would be bad enough, but the humiliation worse. Everyone from the mosque was forced to watch, as if he were a criminal rather than the husband of a loving wife. Fortunately the al-Hisba said 'could' rather than 'will'.

"I'm really sorry about those pictures," Adnan said, while waiting for the stranger from another country to determine his fate. Adnan felt his heart racing while pedestrians hurried to work; cars, busses and taxis filled the roads, and the city seemed normal. But Raqqah was being slaughtered silently. All who lived there knew that, and thanks to a brave group of men on Facebook; the world knew that Raqqah was being slaughtered silently. They had a Facebook group and a website too, with many stories and pictures of the terror inflicted upon the residents of Raqqah. Something Adnan could no long follow, but he was sure they were still posting despite many risks.

"You're coming with me," the al-Hisba said, before grabbing Adnan's arm and guiding him through the crush. Everybody avoided eye contact while the al-Hisba took Adnan to the Black Stadium; the Raqqah football stadium built in distinctive, dark concrete. Through the opening to the playing field, now bare and dusty with items of DAESH brutality scattered about. Blocks for beheadings stood on earth stained with blood, and there were crude, steel crosses too. Adnan shuddered. Was that to be his fate for having pictures of Ranim? Was he to be killed in that stadium, where once he followed the home games of al-Shabab?

A commotion to the left, where two DAESH forced a man, perhaps in his 30s, along one of the player's races to the field. Adnan watched as they took that man to a block and forced him to kneel in the way every man living in Raqqah recognised. In the near-silent stadium, one DAESH swung a sword and that man was killed. Just like that. More blood drained onto the field, before they dragged his remains away.

Momentarily Adnan wondered where DAESH buried their many victims. In DAESH eyes their victims were unworthy Muslims, so probably in unmarked graves beyond the outskirts.

The al-Hisba guided Adnan to that player's race, where they went down a ramp to a green-painted corridor beneath the stadium. Many doors led off that corridor, and through an open door Adnan saw a man shackled by his wrists to chains hanging from a concrete beam, and a second man strapped to a steel bed frame. An al-Hisba touched two wires to that frame, and that poor man screamed as electricity was sent through his body. Adnan felt even sicker; soon he would be tortured.

From many rooms off that green corridor, men shouted and screamed and bellowed. The Black Stadium was a torture chamber of gigantic proportions. Adnan was led into a room which had a man hanging from his wrists, while a DAESH pummelled him with a tyre on a rope. That poor man grunted loudly each time the heavy tyre hit him. Adnan knew he would be tortured, although he wondered why. He wondered why DAESH tortured men when they could just execute them and get it over with. Adnan knew he was going to die at the hands of those barbarians, and the worst thing was he never had a chance to say goodbye to Ranim, and to say goodbye to his family. He loved them and now he was going to leave this world without telling them that. At first they would wonder where he'd gone, until after a time they would guess that DAESH killed him. Forever they would wonder what happened and why. In that room, Adnan didn't understand what was happening and why. Why did he have to die?

"Who do you have, Man?" a voice asked, and Adnan turned to face the al-Hisba with the tyre.

"What's your name?" the first al-Hisba asked.

"Adnan Richie," Adnan said.

"He has obscene pictures on his phone."

"Let me see," the al-Hisba with the tyre said.

The phone was handed across, and the al-Hisba with the tyre casually flicked through the pictures by using his thumb.

"Who's this?" he asked.

"My wife," Adnan said. "She wanted me to be aroused for her when I come home from work."

"She's beautiful. You're a lucky man. Why did you bring him, Man?"

"Because of those pictures," the first al-Hisba said.

"Of his wife on their marriage bed? Stupid idiot," he muttered. He shoved the phone at Adnan who put it in his pocket. "Where do you work?"

"My father has a cafe," Adnan said.

"Delete those pictures in case some other idiot gets the same idea, and go to work at your father's cafe." He got up close and whispered in Adnan's ear. "Your wife's smiling brightly and it's clear she loves you a lot. I'm not going to torture and kill a man for love."

Adnan nodded, but couldn't bring himself to say the words 'thank you'.

"Make sure you're at midday prayers," the al-Hisba with the tyre said

Adnan nodded again, before heading along that corridor of pain, up the race, across the field soaked with blood, and through the entrance to freedom. There he paused. He could have been tortured and executed. Just metres away, beneath the stadium, men were being tortured before execution. He and Ranim had to leave Raqqah, now. But first he had to get to work, because Papa would be worried. He took a deep breath and headed into crowds of men heading to many jobs across the city. Shortly after, Adnan reached Cafe Hamid and greeted Papa.

"What's wrong?" Papa asked.

Adnan paused while he thought about what to say. He felt embarrassed about those pictures of Ranim. "An al-Hisba looked at my phone and got the wrong idea about something, so he took me to the Black Stadium. DAESH have a torture chamber...."

"A torture chamber?" Papa interrupted.

"A massive torture chamber under the stadium," Adnan said. "They torture men and execute them, but fortunately they realised their mistake and let me go."

Papa grabbed Adnan's shoulders and looked him in his eyes. "Are you alright?"

"I'm fine."

"No you're not. You should go home."

"I'd prefer to be busy at work, rather than worrying Ranim with my problems."

"I understand." Papa drew a deep breath. "We should all leave Raqqah but we can't."

"Why not?" Adnan asked.

"DAESH won't allow women under the age of thirty to leave Raqqah, so you can't leave because of Ranim and we can't leave because of Lina."

"When did this happen?"

"Just the other day."

"That's bad."

"I know. Be careful with your phone."

"I fixed it."

"Good. What was the problem, so I can tell my friends,"

"Ah...," Adnan said while he thought of what to say. "I had pictures of Ranim."

"Just pictures?"

"Pictures of Ranim naked."

"Oh."

"Don't tell anyone."

"I won't. Papa hugged Adnan. "You're a good man Adnan, and I'm sure Ranim knows how lucky she is."

Adnan nodded.

"I must get things ready," Papa said, before he went to the kitchen.

Adnan leaned against the counter with his arms crossed while he pondered Cafe Hamid. It was long and narrow, with timber tables and timber chairs to the right, and the dark, timber counter to the left, complete with a coffee machine and a glass display cabinet for cakes and pastries. Past the counter the cafe widened, with red cloth-covered seats for customers to sit, relax and smoke hookahs. The paintwork was dark burgundy, and while some light came through the large window, most light came from lights above each table. Behind the counter was the kitchen where Adnan's father worked, while Adnan managed sales and serving.

Adnan set to taking the two black, metal tables and four white, plastic chairs outside onto the footpath. Papa was generous with his pay increase, but since Ranim was unable to work, Adnan's finances had tightened. He couldn't ask Papa for more money, because they lost many customers through the ban on smoking. Once men came to cafes to drink coffee, smoke, and talk with their friends, but now men stayed home to smoke and drink coffee in safety.

Adnan put a lot of effort into serving customers efficiently and politely, even DAESH customers, because tips helped. Despite having fewer customers, those tips helped a lot, except on Friday when they had to close and go to prayers at midday. Businesspeople who were devout used to pray in their shops and offices, but for the past months al-Hisba made sure every business was closed and all men went to a mosque. That cost even more business for the cafe, because they couldn't make money when closed for more than an hour.

Adnan waited for customers, while wondering why DAESH inflicted such cruelty on the people they'd conquered. It was impossible to turn the calendar back to the time of Prophet Muhammad, peace be upon him, because there'd been too much change since then. And why would they bother, and with such zeal? Did they really believe the path to God was from more than a thousand years ago? Did they really believe the path to God came from torture and execution? Adnan couldn't understand the motives of DAESH or their followers, who mostly came from Saudi Arabia, Tunisia, Egypt, and other places; even Australia.

After a steady Friday morning and a few tips, the call for prayer echoed across the city. Papa locked the cafe before they headed to Abdullah bin Masood mosque.

Crowds of men swarmed to the mosque, hurriedly removing their shoes before queuing to wash hands and faces, and then each man stood by a prayer mat inside. Usually the ritual of prayer soothed Adnan, but not that day. He came close to being tortured and executed, and he couldn't keep his thoughts from that. After prayer they had to go outside where seven men were stripped to the waist, before they received 40 lashes each for crimes ranging from smoking to listening to music. There were no executions that day; usually shot in the head but sometimes beheaded in public, so Adnan returned to Cafe Hamid with Papa.

The afternoon passed with Adnan still far away. How could they continue to live in a city where the most innocent of acts were crimes? Was there another way? Not that Adnan could think of.

Adnan was surprised when Papa turned the open / closed sign on the door. The working day was over and it was time to go home. He bid Papa ma'a as-salaama, before heading home. Just along was the park, which unusually had a pile of rock recently dumped. Some men went to inspect that rock, which was a curious sight. Adnan wasn't interested, but he was caught amongst the crowd descending on the park. A little further in, he saw four DAESH with faces concealed by black hoods, and holding rifles. He went to skirt around them, but dark looks from their eyes showed he should remain in the crowd.

A woman; dressed in black but not wearing a niqab, was led to a small hole by two more DAESH with hoods, and made to climb in. An imam announced that Faddah al-Sayed Ahmad was guilty of adultery, and her penalty was to be stoned to death. All that was visible was the poor woman's head, and even if she committed adultery, which probably was pre-marital sex with her intended husband, she didn't deserve to die, and never like that. One of the DAESH shouted at the crowd to carry out the sentence, but none moved. Another shouted but still there was no movement. Then four DAESH threw the rocks at that woman, rocks that were small enough to be thrown easily but large enough to inflict terrible injuries. Adnan expected the poor woman to cry out in pain, but she was silent. Probably she was praying because her mortal life was ending. With fervent vigour those four DAESH threw rocks while Adnan looked to leave, but two more DAESH watched over all who were there. The face of Faddah al-Sayed was reduced to a bloody pulp as each stone brutalised her more and more; until she was no longer recognisable as a woman or even as a human. Still they threw stones until surely she was dead, and that was the end of it. The crowd was eerily silent when one of the DAESH signalled they could leave. Adnan left with a heaving stomach and a heavy heart.

He went home, went upstairs, unlocked the door and went inside. Ranim greeted him but Adnan found it hard to even respond. Still his stomach churned, while he felt very, very sad.

"What's wrong my love?" Ranim asked.

Adnan looked into her face. "I had a bad day," he said wearily. "First they took my phone and he saw the pictures we took. I got into trouble for that," Adnan said, but he didn't want to worry Ranim about how serious that trouble was.

"I'm sorry," Ranim said. "I should never have asked you to take them."

He held her hands. "That's not your fault," he said. "You love me and you wanted to share a special gift with me. A personal and intimate gift, just for me. I thank you a thousand times, a million times, for such a wonderful gift. But that's not all. On the way home they guided us to a park, where they stoned a woman to death for adultery."

Ranim gasped and put her hands over her mouth.

"They wanted us to throw stones, but nobody did," Adnan said. "So they did it instead. But we couldn't leave until it was over."

Ranim hugged him, and he hugged her too. She felt good.

"I'm sorry you had to see that," Ranim said.

"We can't go on like this," Adnan said.

"What can we do?"

"I don't know. I would leave Raqqah but we can't."

"Why not?"

"They won't let women under the age of thirty, leave."

Ranim put her hands to her cheeks. "That's bad," she said.

"I know."

"You're a sensitive man Adnan, and that's what I love about you. I don't want to be locked inside, or only allowed out when I'm covered all over, but we just have to make do with life as it is."

"Is there going to be an end to this?" Adnan asked rhetorically.

"The end of this will come from Assad's army."

Adnan pondered that they had gone a full circle, with their saviour being the man they once wanted to be rid of. How stupid and pointless was that?

"Come my love," Ranim said. "We should eat. Tomorrow's Saturday, and we must go out together. Tomorrow will be a better day, I promise."

Adnan remembered those moments in that room beneath the Black Stadium, when everything seemed too late.

"Ranim," Adnan said. "I love you."

"I love you too," she said.

"No!" Adnan exclaimed. "I really, really love you."

"I know you love me, and I really, really love you too."

Chapter Eight

There was a Facebook group: Raqqah is Being Slaughtered Silently, which Sarya browsed from time to time. They posted about life under DAESH which horrified her. Simple things like women not allowed out of their homes alone, to beheadings and crucifixions for minor offences. DAESH boasted of their brutality, especially against homosexual men. DAESH posted videos, which Sarya found through Twitter on #daesh, of how they killed homosexual men by throwing them from the rooves of tall buildings. She discussed some of these things on Twitter, and was grateful that she was proficient enough in English to do that. Her Papa was right when he said English would connect her to the rest of the world.

At that moment the YPG and the YPJ were fighting DAESH at Kobanî. Unless DAESH was stopped they could overrun Rojava, and turn Rojavan lives into what was happening in Raqqah. DAESH would destroy the Charter of the Social Contract and turn women into nobodies; locked at home or only able to go out when escorted by another woman or a male guardian. The priority for all Kurds must be to stop DAESH. But Sarya had to wait until the end of school next year, which might be too late.

That day at school they talked about Kobanî, which made Sarya more impatient to join the YPJ. She was still thinking about that after school, while they headed out the gate.

"You're far from us today," Gulan said.

Sarya knew she was. "I've been thinking about DAESH fighting us at Kobanî, and what would happen if we lose."

"I hope we don't lose."

"Have you ever thought of joining the cause?" Sarya asked.

"Have you?" Gulan asked.

"My parents said I can join the YPJ when I finish school."

"They did!" Dila exclaimed.

"Yes they did," Sarya said. "As long as I finish school."

Medya frowned. "I could do that," she said.

"Me too," Dila said. "If my parents let me."

"You should ask your parents," Sarya said. "You should tell them that my Mama and my Papa want me to join the YPJ when I finish school. That might encourage your parents to give you their blessings to join the YPJ."

"Your father is headmaster and well-respected, and if he lets you go to war then my parents will let me go to war too."

"That's true," Gulan said.

Sarya knew what they should do. "When school finishes next year," she said. "We can all join together."

"We can join together, and we can fight together too," Gulan said.

"Enough of this talk about fighting!" Medya exclaimed. "Who's going to Berma's party tomorrow?"

Much commotion, and they all were going.

"I need new shoes," Sarya said; looking down at her school shoes which were old and battered.

"We'll go shopping together for your shoes," Gulan said.

Sarya looped her hand through Gulan's arm. "We'll both go shopping," she said.

They all headed away together, to separate a little further on for their respective homes.

* * *

Spring blossoms brightened the many parks of Raqqah. But the streets of Raqqah were dull and grey as life rapidly became intolerable, and that showed on everyone's faces, except their DAESH masters, the men and women of al-Hisba; the religious police. Al-Hisba were ready in a moment to persecute citizens of Raqqah for the most minor of transgressions, but that wasn't the only problem. There were four or five hours of blackouts a day, and shortages of basic foods. Ranim and their neighbour Nour queued together to buy expensive bread for a day. The price of gas soared to about fifty pounds a cylinder, so they avoided cooked meals as much as possible. Many families turned to wood for cooking, and it was as if Raqqah had returned to a past age.

But they were trapped in Raqqah, and with the cafe losing money, Adnan felt like a burden on his family. With high prices and exorbitant taxes, only DAESH militants had money to spend in cafes. With so few customers, Adnan's father could run the cafe on his own. Adnan could join DAESH because they paid good wages, and many young men joined DAESH for the money, but Adnan would rather starve than do that. There had to be something though.

"I should leave the cafe and get another job," Adnan said over breakfast of yesterday's bread with a little honey, and a cup of tea. He didn't know what, and then he did. "People have started using firewood to cook," he said. "I'll ask the firewood merchants for a job, and even if I earn just a little, that'll help everyone."

"We should have left when we could," Ranim said glumly.

"We didn't know things would go this bad, and now they won't let women your age leave Raqqah."

"I know; but I wish we could have a family.

Having children was a bad idea. "If we have a daughter; she won't be allowed to go to school, and even though we could teach her at home, that isn't the same. But if we have a son he'll be brainwashed into being a DAESH militant, and even brainwashed into committing suicide attacks if they want him to. When the time is right we can have children, but I don't want to have our son turned into a DAESH militant, or have our son turn us in to be executed for apostasy, which we know has happened to some parents."

Ranim sighed, and Adnan knew she wished they had left when they could.

"I need to find a job," Adnan said. "As long as we have enough money to pay our rent and buy food; then we'll get by until things get better."

Ranim still looked sad.

"Things will get better," Adnan said, but he didn't believe that either.

After breakfast, Adnan headed towards the sheep market, where firewood vendors operated. He went to the first merchant who sweated while he unloaded a battered, olive green, Bedford truck. He was in his forties and a bit pudgy; working hard on a sunny, spring morning

"Sabaah al-khayr," Adnan greeted. "My name's Adnan Richie and I'm looking for work."

"Sabaah al-khayr," the man replied, while he wiped his brow with a handkerchief. "My name's Abdul Farzat, and I can't afford to pay you much."

"I can work for anything reasonable."

"One thousand pounds a day?"

That was reasonable. "Yes; one thousand pounds a day."

"Good. Help me unload, and help when our customers come."

"I used to work in a cafe."

"That will be useful."

"Can I make a call first?" Adnan asked.

"Of course."

Adnan went to his contacts and rang Papa's mobile. That became difficult because Papa felt he'd let his son down, but Adnan assured Papa that when things got better, he would return to the cafe. Papa accepted that, and Adnan wished ma'a as-salaama and hung up.

Adnan then climbed into the truck, and tossed the cut branches of timber into a heap on the ground. Then he was told to stack that heap neatly, by which time customers were dealing with Ustaaz Farzat. Adnan was asked to deliver bundles of wood for older customers, and he worked quite hard for several hours. At the end, Ustaaz Farzat gave Adnan two banknotes, and Adnan thanked him.

"Come here tomorrow morning at seven," Ustaaz Farzat said.

"I will."

Adnan was pleased that he was no longer a burden on his family, and with one thousand pounds a day, he and Ranim would get by. They would have to be careful with their money, but they would get by.

* * *

While Erna showered, Vache went to the desk in the living room and started his computer. He sipped coffee until he was able to check the news. The main story was DAESH formally announcing the establishment of a worldwide caliphate, with the capital of that caliphate in Raqqah. DAESH leader, al-Abu Bakr Baghdadi, was named caliph, to be known as Caliph Ibrahim, and they renamed themselves from the Islamic State of Iraq and the Levant, to Islamic State. Vache didn't know the formalities of Islam, other than the religion seemed to be fractured into many different factions, and those factions were never in agreement with each other. But for once, on the subject of this caliphate and on al-Abu Bakr Baghdadi, Islam was united in condemnation.

Vache used Wikipedia to discover that a caliphate was a territory under the leadership of a caliph, who was the successor to Prophet Muhammad. No wonder the rest of Islam were united against Baghdadi unilaterally making himself the head of Islam! DAESH was more and more isolated, but they had many fighters, many weapons, including tanks and artillery, and they held substantial territories in Iraq and Syria.

Vache returned to the news, where there were reports that the Kurdish YPG and YPJ were making progress against DAESH at Kobanî. He pondered that. Using Wikipedia once more, he read about the YPG and then backtracked to the Kurdish PYD[3], or the Democratic Union Party. He then went to the YPG website and read their detailed introduction. They wanted a free, democratic and secular Syria, which of course put them at odds with DAESH. The YPG were non-capitalist and non-fascist, and unusually for Islamic people, they were anti-patriarchal. In fact the logo on the page had the image of a woman soldier. Primarily the website was looking for international volunteers in the fight against DAESH.

Vache needed verification though. First he went to The Telegraph in the UK, where there were articles which validated what he felt. They were an effective fighting force, and they were holding ground against DAESH. He then went to The Guardian and read more articles. He sipped his mug of coffee while he pondered their next move.

"You have pictures of soldiers there," Erna said.

"Sit, and we can talk," Vache said.

Erna brought one of the cheap chairs from their kitchen to the desk, and sat opposite.

"The Kurdish Democratic Union Party or the PYD have formed People's Protection Units, which are armies for male soldiers and for female soldiers. Already Assad has unofficially capitulated to the PYD in the north of Syria, which they call Rojava, and which is now mostly Kurdish-

---

[3] PYD – Partiya Yekitiya Demokrat or Democratic Union Party

controlled. This Kurdish army is battling DAESH at Kobanî, with the assistance of a Western coalition led by the United States."

"That is interesting," Erna said. "They have an army for women, which is unusual for an Islamic community."

"The PYD believe in secularism and women's equality, and they have a political and economic manifesto of collectivism. I don't understand the significance of that, but unchecked capitalism invariably leads to inequality and economic chaos, as we've seen with the global financial crisis and its aftermath, so collectivism might be worth trying. Socially, their fighting force is organised on collective lines, and seems to be doing well against DAESH."

"I'm interested in these armies...."

"Although there are two armies," Vache said. "They fight as one force."

"It's novel that women are playing a major part in this war, and I'd like to be a part of that. I'm sure this Kurdish force would appreciate a doctor and a nurse volunteering."

Vache thought that was almost certain. He doubted there was a surplus of doctors and nurses in Rojava, and a twenty-six year old doctor and a twenty-six year old nurse would be welcomed.

"How should we do this?" Erna asked.

Vache turned to his laptop screen, where the YPG contact page had an email address and an encryption mechanism. He turned away. "We should send them an email, to volunteer our services as doctor and nurse."

"They'll accept us; I'm sure. When they do we can give notice to the hospital, pack personal belongings, put the rest in storage not that there's much, arrange our journey, and let our families know."

Vache finished his coffee while thinking that was the path they should take.

Chapter Nine

Kobanî was all but encircled by DAESH, and the only way to the city was through Turkey. Their flight was the reverse of their journey almost exactly 18 months previously. On Wednesday September 10, 2014; they left Amman bound for Istanbul, to change planes to a regional flight to Sanliurfa, arriving just before seven that evening. The next morning they caught a bus to Suruç, and then a taxi towards Kobanî, stopping a few kilometres short of that city just over the border. In the distance was a huddle of concrete buildings on an undulating plain. From there they walked to the war zone, which was a real war zone. Some buildings were intact, some were damaged, and some buildings were reduced to rubble. Men and women soldiers in green camouflage, all carrying automatic rifles, wandered past in small groups. Commercial vehicles, Toyota Landcruisers mostly, had been coopted into military service. Artillery boomed in the distance. The email told them to meet Komutan Uzun, but Vache didn't want to disturb these soldiers.

A woman spoke, and Vache turned to face a young woman in her camouflage uniform and holding a rifle. She looked Kurdish with a deep brown complexion, dark eyes, and her black hair wrapped in a blue scarf. "Do you speak Arabic?" Vache asked.

"I do," she said in Arabic.

"We're looking for Komutan Egîd."

She nodded her head. "Come with me."

Off they went through the main shopping street of badly damaged buildings and a few destroyed cars; dodging rubble from near-ruins in parts. On to what looked like a former professional office, coopted by the military. The young woman soldier led them into an office with a desk, chair and filing cabinet, and spoke with a male soldier at that desk.

"This man is Komutan Egîd," she told Vache.

"Thank you," Vache said.

She nodded and headed away.

"Excuse me," Vache said in Arabic to a soldier at the desk, engrossed with a tablet computer. "We were told to come to Kobanî to see you."

"And you are?"

"I'm Doctor Vache Lang and this is my wife Erna Tavitian, who's a nurse."

"You're volunteering for our cause?"

"This is our cause too," Vache said. "We left Raqqah when DAESH took over, and we've been waiting for our chance to help destroy them."

"That's good," he said with a big smile. "Sit please."

They sat opposite the komutan, or 'commander' in Kurdish. He wore no fancy marks on his uniform, and could have been one of the soldiers outside.

97

"We're of Armenian ancestry," Erna said. "For a century our families have lived in Syria, which we call home."

"Armenians are stateless like us," Komutan Egîd said.

"There's an Armenian homeland, but not for Western Armenians like us. So yes, we're stateless like you."

"I'll give you a quick briefing. The YPG and the YPJ are equivalent to brigades, and beneath that we have battalions or tabûra, and teams or kom; and a leader is a komutan, or commander in Kurdish, regardless of brigade, battalion or team. Above team level we have co-commanders; one man and one woman, while men or women can command teams. We make no distinction between men and women in our society, and if I had the time I would tell you more about our beliefs, which go beyond Western feminism to true equality of the sexes. Everyone else in our forces is comrade, or havel in Kurdish. So you'll be Pizisk Vache for Doctor Vache, and Havel Erna, for Comrade Erna. A doctor and a nurse are going to be helpful to us, and you can work from field hospitals near our front lines. We're a mobile force so hospitals are temporary, and you'll have to make the best of what we can provide."

Vache pondered that.

"We work as small teams, with a komutan leading," Komutan Egîd said. "We encourage ideas from all comrades: men and women. We have team meetings called tekmil, for constructive critique of each other and of their commanders."

98

That sounded interesting. That sounded really interesting for an army.

"Another thing you should know is sexual relations between our soldiers are proscribed, to avoid any form of sexual harassment," Komutan Egîd said. "Being husband and wife that won't apply to you two, but please be discreet."

Komutan Egîd then stood. "Come with me and we'll get you started," he said, while he headed out the door. Vache and Erna followed to a white Toyota Landcruiser utility with several soldiers of both sexes seated at the rear; talking loudly in Kurdish. Komutan Egîd spoke with the driver before gesturing for Vache and Erna to climb on. They joined the noisy throng, but cradling backpacks and a medical bag rather than AK47s. A roar from the diesel engine and they were on their way to the front lines of the battle with DAESH.

In no time they left the ruins of Kobanî behind, to bounce along a narrow and potholed road while closing on booming artillery. Surrounded by cheerful young soldiers singing Kurdish songs, and behaving like they were going to a picnic rather than going to war, Vache felt uplifted. These people would defeat DAESH, he was sure of it, and he was going to be a part of that.

PART TWO

Chapter Ten

It was a cold February day. February the 3rd, 2015; after more than a year of the DAESH rule of Raqqah. On his way home from work, Adnan was surprised to see a large television screen on a trailer, and even more surprised to see DAESH al-Hisba shepherding men to stand in front of this screen. Adnan wasn't interested in watching their cruelty and barbarism, like the time he was forced to watch that terrible stoning, so he headed along a side street instead. There an al-Hisba told Adnan to go to the screen, in typically Saudi Arabian-accented Arabic. Adnan avoided eye contact; that was always safer, and returned to the screen. There several al-Hisba stood at the perimeter of the crowd with their rifles ready, while the video began. At first Adnan was quite confused until the film showed a Jordanian official talking about their pilots; then Adnan remembered the Jordanian pilot, Muath al-Kasasbeh, who ejected when the engine of his aircraft failed, and he was captured by DAESH. For a time the film berated Jordan for their campaign against DAESH, with a backdrop of Jordanian soldiers in battle, before the film had an extract from Jordanian television news of their pilot being captured.

Then the captured pilot dressed in simple, orange overalls, talked about what he did to DAESH while flying his aircraft, and also what his country, Jordan, did to DAESH.

The film cut to the desert where the pilot, still dressed in orange overalls, walked across dry, dusty ground, interspersed with images of aircraft and injured people. Then, surrounded by DAESH in sand-coloured camouflage, with evil faces hidden behind black masks, Muath al-Kasasbeh was shown locked in a cage; praying while standing. A DAESH soldier also with a mask, although it was an insult to real soldiers to call him that, lit a trail of flammable material which slowly crept to the cage. Adnan wanted to turn away but he knew many eyes were on him, and on all men in the crowd, so he had to watch their barbarity. He couldn't drop his eyes even, so Adnan tried to calm his mind as the cage erupted in flames and the poor pilot tried vainly to protect himself from that horrific conflagration. For what seemed an eternity Muath al-Kasasbeh was alive and burning; frantically beating at flames consuming him, but he had no chance because that fire was too intense. The poor, poor pilot desperately beat at the inferno which engulfed him, before he collapsed to his knees. Flames burned high while dramatic music played, with spoken words proclaiming their sick, twisted views about Islam. Muath al-Kasasbeh eventually fell into a heap; clearly dead. Then DAESH dumped dirt on the cage with a tractor before running it over and destroying his remains.

Adnan was shocked and confused, while the crowd around him, also too scared turn away, were eerily silent. Adnan wondered what type of men would even contemplate doing such a thing. Adnan wanted to go home that moment and talk to Ranim. He had to talk with Ranim to let the shock out; that's what it was; he had to let his shock out. He headed to their apartment to tell Ranim what he'd been forced to watch. He had to hear her soothing voice and be calmed by her. Adnan walked briskly while terrified that DAESH would be suspicious of his haste. Every waking moment he had to be alert and on guard because of those monsters of men and the dreadful, inhumane things they did.

Adnan raced up the staircase, and fumbled at the lock on their door before he was able to get inside.

"Adnan!" Ranim exclaimed. "What happened?"

"On the way home from work, DAESH made us watch a video of that Jordanian pilot being burned to death," Adnan blurted out.

She put her hands to her mouth. "Oh, I'm so sorry my love." She came to him and hugged him. "That must have been terrible."

Adnan hugged her too, and he felt like a great weight was lifted from his soul.

"I'm so sorry my love," she said again. "If I could take what you saw away, I would."

"You're taking my pain away now," Adnan murmured.

"I love you so much and I don't want you to get hurt."

"I don't want to see you hurt by DAESH either."

"I'm not so bad. Nour and I go out together, and going out during the day means a lot to me, and means a lot to Nour too. Once we were neighbours and now we're good friends, all because of DAESH."

Adnan felt even better. No much how much DAESH tried to grind them down; goodness always rose to the surface.

"What do you want me to do?" Ranim asked.

"Just hold me," Adnan murmured.

"I love you," she said.

"I love you too."

"Love will overcome hate."

"Always."

* * *

Jordan turned on DAESH for what they did to one of their own. Two days later on Thursday, airstrikes began just out of Raqqah, the capital of DAESH. That wasn't the first time Raqqah was targeted by airstrikes, but they were the closest and the most prolonged. Day and night buildings, probably targets specific to DAESH, were pounded as Jordan unleashed her fury. Adnan thought he knew airstrikes but that was different. That was close and that was dangerous. That was really dangerous. Life in Raqqah ground to a halt. Businesses closed; Adnan stayed home because the sheep market was in the open, and surely Abdul stayed home too. While that fury raged, Ranim said they should do something special when it was over. Adnan wondered if those airstrikes ever would be over, but after three days of terror, Jordan's wrath was satiated.

"What special thing do you want to do, my love?" Adnan asked.

"What's the most important thing in the world?" Ranim asked.

"Family."

"I want to visit my family."

That was a great idea. After a phone call, lunch was arranged for the next day.

Adnan hated having to escort his wife covered in black from head to toe, and she even had to wear black gloves. Ranim was beautiful and he was proud of her beauty, and always she dressed tastefully and fashionably. But now she was reduced to – black, as if he was her master and she was his slave. In their marriage he wanted them to be equals, which they were until they went outside together.

They reached her parent's apartment, where Papa Fakhri invited them both in. As soon as Ranim crossed the threshold, she tore her black robe and face scarf off, and her gloves too, to reveal a lovely white blouse and blue skirt.

She tossed all that blackness on the floor, before kissing her parents and her younger brother Saami.

"How are you all?" Ranim asked.

"Good to see you my daughter," Papa Fakhri said. "I only wish life was as good for your marriage, as life was when we first got married."

Ranim took Adnan's hand. "We love each other, and our love overcomes the hatred around us."

Adnan then realised something. "Did you realise under DAESH; you and I could never have courted and married?"

Ranim looked at him. "Yes, you're right," she eventually said. She looked towards her father. "That makes us very lucky."

"That makes you very lucky," Mama Fakhri echoed. "I know how much you love each other, and I believe you when you say your love overcomes this hatred around us all."

"This will be over one day," Adnan said.

"How?'

"The Kurdish army will defeat DAESH," Adnan said; recalling what he saw on the internet about the Kurdish victory at Kobane.

"Do you think they can do that?"

"They've beaten DAESH already, and they have the American airforce on their side."

"I hope the Kurdish army will defeat DAESH," Papa Fakhri said.

"Enough talk of DAESH!" Mama Fakhri said. "Let's eat!"

"I can help you serve," Ranim said, and went with her mother.

"How are you in your job, Adnan?" Papa Fakhri asked.

"I'm doing well," Adnan said. "When the cafe comes good I'll return there, but for now we're doing well."

"That's good to hear. When you asked me, one thing I knew for certain was that Ranim was in good hands, and you were going to be happy together. Sorry," he smiled brightly. "That's two things. In any case we've gained a son rather than losing a daughter, and that's good for us all."

"Come on you two," Ranim said. "This food will get cold."

They went to the dining area where Mama Fakhri had put on a veritable feast. Good fortune worked both ways. It was like Adnan had gained another father and another mother, which was good for them all. He sat beside Ranim, and contemplated which tasty-looking dish to start with.

"We had good fortune," Ranim said. "What about those who come after?"

Adnan didn't quite know what she meant, and then he did.

"There can only be arranged marriages," Papa Fakhri said. "Arranged marriages are only a means of introduction, and it's up to the couple to agree or not."

"What about Saami and Lina?'

107

Papa Fakhri frowned. "Sammi's only nineteen. How old is Lina?"

"Twenty-one," Adnan said.

"That might work," Papa Fakhri said.

"Saami's a bit like me, and Lina's a bit like Adnan," Ranim said.

"Don't I get a say?" Saami asked.

"Of course you do!" Mama Fakhri exclaimed. "Women can't go out these days, so the only way you can meet a bride is through an introduction, like being introduced to Lina, who you've met a few times already."

"There's no rush," Papa Fakhri said. "Saami's only nineteen. But in a year or two, we'll arrange for Saami and Lina to have time together, and real time together with no chaperones, however we can arrange that."

"Lina's room in her apartment, or Saami's room here," Ranim said.

"Yes; that would work."

Adnan thought that would work well, when the time came for it. Two years age difference and similar backgrounds might make them a good match, when it was time for that.

* * *

Raqqah was isolated from the rest of the world, except for the internet. There were many good things in marriage, especially spending time together after a day at work, but Adnan also liked to keep up to date with world events each day. In particular, what was happening elsewhere in Raqqah, and also the war between Kurds and DAESH. That was quite interesting given many Kurdish women, Muslim Kurdish women, were in their army and fighting DAESH. DAESH hated women and now they were being killed by women.

After dinner, Adnan went to his smartphone to quickly catch up on the latest. He was surprised that he had a phone signal but no internet connection.

"Have you tried the internet today?" he asked Ranim.

"I have, but I couldn't get through," Ranim said. "Syriatel must have problems. That's a pity because I like to keep in touch with my friends through Facebook, which I can't easily do face to face."

Adnan put his phone on the small table. They had a television but there were no programs, and now he didn't have the internet. "I wonder what we can do to pass the time?" Adnan thought out loud.

Ranim laughed. "We've been married for more than three years now."

"And?"

She tweaked his nose. "I don't think your desire's ever going to fade," and then she kissed his cheek.

Adnan thought there was no reason they couldn't love each other with passion in 20 or even 30 year's time. "Are you interested?" he asked.

Ranim stood and unbuttoned her blouse, while Adnan watched her. She knew he liked to watch her. Her blouse was removed and her slacks too, tight over her broad hips. Then her white bra revealing her magnificent breasts, nipples already swollen, and her white panties revealing her discreet essence of femininity. She took his hand and led him to their bedroom.

* * *

Adnan lay on his back while Ranim curled into his side.

"I love the way you're exhausted after making love," she said quietly. She put her arm across his chest. "I've drained you of your strength, and now you have to recover."

"Let's sleep, just like this," Adnan said.

"That will be nice."

The next morning, Adnan tried his smartphone once more, but still there was no internet. He frowned. He rang Syriatel but their number was engaged, and he had to get to work.

"My love," he said. "Can you ring Syriatel and find out what's happened to the internet?"

"Of course," she said.

It was a hot, summer's day, and through the day Adnan dreamed of getting home and freshening himself with a shower. He did just that, and while showering he remembered. After dressing in a fresh t-shirt and a pair of trousers, he went to their living room and sat on the couch.

"Did you get through to Syriatel?" he asked.

"I did and its bad news," Ranim said. "DAESH have cut the internet off."

"Pardon?" Adnan asked; surprised.

"They've cut the internet off to Raqqah, but Syriatel told me internet cafes are still working."

"That's a different sort of internet by cable."

Ranim sat beside him. "I like catching up with my friends on Facebook during the day, but now I can't. I can go with Nour to a cafe and we can both catch up with our friends, but we can't do that every day."

She looked so sad and that broke Adnan's heart.

"Come here," he said, and she put her head on his chest. "I'm sorry my love," he said quietly while he hugged her lightly.

"I miss not having the internet at home," Ranim said. "Sometimes I would get a thought, and then I could follow that through. Like when I discovered where DAESH came from."

Adnan was startled. "Where did DAESH come from?" he asked.

"DAESH has been around for a while, but it really comes from the war in Iraq by America, Britain and Australia. That war ended the power held by the Sunni minority in Iraq, in favour of the Shia majority there. From that came the Islamic State of Iraq, who were Sunni Muslims who were upset their power was destroyed by those Western countries. The Islamic State of Iraq recruited army commanders who'd been taken out of the Iraqi army by America, put in prison for a while, and then released. The Islamic State of Iraq then became the Islamic State of Iraq and the Levant, or DAESH. DAESH is a good army to win so much of Syria and Iraq, and those commanders must be the reason why they're so good."

"Western meddling," Adnan grumbled.

"Yes it was."

It was always Western meddling. When would they ever learn?

Chapter Eleven

Sarya came home clutching the plastic shopping bag. She went inside to greet Mama before heading to her room. She laid the polyester, green camouflage-patterned uniform on her bed and pondered it. Sarya went to her chest and carefully emptied her clothes until she found the scarf she wanted. She laid that dark green patterned scarf on the uniform, and then put her black Adidas trainers beside it. Satisfied, she stripped to her underwear before dressing in her uniform, and then pulled on her shoes and tied long laces. Using the mirror on the back of her door, she tied the green scarf over head and around her long, braided ponytail. She contemplated that for a moment, before going to the living room. Just then the door opened and Papa came through. He stopped for a moment with his eyes wide, and then grabbed Sarya's shoulders and looked her in the eyes.

"You look like a real soldier," he said.

"Thank you Papa," Sarya replied.

"My little girl does look like a soldier," Mama said, before hugging Sarya.

"Thank you Mama," Sarya said, while feeling her eyes moisten.

"When do you leave for training?" Papa asked.

"Tomorrow morning at six. Gulan, Dila, Medya and I."

"I'll get up early to prepare a proper breakfast," Mama said.

Sarya appreciated that, and she knew they would see her off too.

"I'll change my clothes," Sarya said.

She went to her room to put on her civilian clothes for the last time, and returned to the kitchen to help Mama prepare dinner. That was a quiet dinner while Sarya sensed they all had many thoughts. She was thinking about her training to come, and war to follow, while her parents wondered if they would ever see her again.

Early the next morning was cool for a late June day, so Sarya pulled a dark grey windcheater over her uniform before they set off for the YPG and YPJ recruitment office in the centre of town. There, Gulan, Dila and Medya waited with their families, along with Zinet from the recruitment office. The diesel engine of a white Toyota Landcruiser rattled noisily while the girls bid their families goodbye. Three in the back and Sarya in the front, before they headed out of Amûdê and turned south towards DAESH. After two hour's driving they reached a small village, like many small villages in that area, but protected by an earth bank bulldozed around the perimeter. There was a break in the bank for the entrance to the training camp, complete with a gate, and this had a sign: Martyr Zera, and the girl's picture. They drove into the abandoned village where a woman in her 30s waited. She kissed each girl three times before telling them that she was Komutan Rosnan, and she would be training Sarya and her friends, and 15 other girls, over the next month.

The abandoned and lonely village on the plains of northern Syria had about 20 simple houses built of concrete bricks, all with flat rooves; much like houses in Amûdê and the house Sarya called home. Only most windows were blown out, much of the furniture had disappeared, and everything was dusty underfoot. One day inhabitants would return, clean their homes, replace carpets and rugs, fix their windows, and life would go on. In the meantime that abandoned village, five kilometres from the front line, was part of the battle against DAESH.

Sarya, Gulan, Dila and Medya were each assigned a mattress on the floor of an abandoned house. It was still cool when they were introduced to the fifteen girls already there. They all sat in a circle in the largest house of the village, where each girl gave her name, age, and what she wanted to do in life. As Sarya expected some of these girls were 16, and joined the YPJ for the freedom and opportunities it offered. Until just a few years ago, the lot of a Kurdish woman was to marry and become the property of her husband, so the YPJ was freedom to these girls. Not unexpectedly most wanted to be teachers. Sarya listened to their tales, some of running away from home, while she remembered what her father once told her. People know nothing about life but home and school, so when the time comes to decide their careers, they pick that which they know, which is school, to become teachers. Most of the girls came from farming families, and farmers were always poor.

Last in the circle was Sarya. "My name's Sarya Goran," she said. "My father's a headmaster in Amûdê. In Rojava we've created a new order of equality between men and women, and equality between the different races who live here: Kurd, Assyrian, Armenian and Arab. DAESH want to destroy our new order, so I joined the YPJ to protect our new way of life. I don't know what to do for the rest of my life just yet, but when I decide my future it will be to help our people."

There was silence for a moment before Komutan Rosnan said, "very good Sarya, and very well thought out. Also, you've introduced us to the next part of this lesson, which is about DAESH and their ambitions for Rojava."

Only then did Sarya realise some of these girls from poor, farming families didn't have smartphones or ready access to the internet, and they mainly saw the YPJ as a way to have different lives to their mothers.

Komutan Rosnan went on to explain the philosophy of DAESH in more detail, and the impact DAESH would have on Rojava if they weren't stopped. One thing in particular struck Sarya: DAESH terrorists believed if they were killed by a woman, they would go to hell. She wondered what impact that would have on their morale. At the very least she would always wear her green scarf tied over her head, so DAESH terrorists knew there they were facing a woman. After that discussion the girls were told to cook lunch, while Komutan Rosnan took Sarya aside.

"You've been keeping up with the war?" Rosnan asked.

"I have a smartphone which I bought from money I made from part-time work," Sarya said. "I know I don't have to join the YPJ to have freedom, but I do know we have to stop DAESH, and I can't sit to one side while others do that."

"I understand."

Sarya helped carry their lunch dishes, and after eating lunch and washing their plates, they were put through an exercise drill, complete with much laughter. Although it was early, Sarya was tired by the time they had dinner, and she had no trouble falling asleep on her mattress in the room shared with Gulan, Dila and Medya.

The next morning after breakfast, Sarya was told to stand while Rosnan draped what she called a flak jacket over her uniform. Rosnan explained that this heavy green jacket had two grenades, four full magazines, a bandage and a tourniquet. Sarya was then given a rifle, which she knew was a Chinese-made AK47 Kalashnikov. All the girls were given flak jackets and rifles, before a long day of parade ground exercises. After lunch they sang songs, the same songs they once sung in Amûdê, and Sarya started to feel a bond of love with these girls from poor, farming families. After all, they were destined to destroy DAESH together.

The following morning after breakfast, they sat in a circle for their first tekmil. Sarya stood when it was her turn, where Daria offered the feedback that Sarya kept her inner feelings to herself. Gulan then stood and said that she'd known Sarya for many years. Sarya was her best friend, and she would lay down her life for her comrades, if necessary. Sarya responded that just because a person is quiet doesn't mean they don't have strong feelings for their comrades. While she said that, she never expected tekmil to be as confronting as it was.

After that, Komutan Rosnan talked about jineology. She explained that when civilisation advanced over time, humankind lost much of its communitarian life, with men becoming soldiers, priests, artisans, and also masters over women. Women could only recover equality through the re-introduction of communitarian lives, which was different to Western feminism, where women attempted to reach equality in a hierarchically structured competitive society that automatically favoured men. Capitalism was inherently anti-woman so jineology was inherently anti-capitalism. Sarya partly understood, and thought jineology was re-shaping society away from that which was comfortable only for men, to something which was comfortable for both men and for women. In any case, she was glad when that discussion ended, and Komutan Rosnan said they were going to discuss democratic confederalism, or as Komutan Rosnan said: there's no point in fighting unless you know what you're fighting for. Sarya remembered her discussion on democratic confederalism at school, and later that evening with her father. But there was always something to be learned. As the YPG and the YPJ liberated villages, towns and cities from DAESH, the PYD helped villagers to elect their commune councils, and helped groups of villages to elect their neighbourhood councils. What Sarya volunteered for was more than a war to defeat DAESH. Theirs was not a war to take over another country, but rather to leave peace and harmony, regardless of race, religion and gender. She was amused by the looks on the other girl's faces, as they realised that as soldiers, they were bringing the gift of peace and self-government to Syria.

* * *

Sarya finished sewing the patch onto the sleeve of her uniform, and pulled the thread tight to cut it with her teeth.

"Who's that?" Gulan asked about the patch, with Dila and Medya peering over Gulan's shoulder.

"Abdullah Öcalan," Sarya said to a blank look. "He invented jineology and democratic confederalism."

Gulan looked even more confused, while Sarya stood to pull on her uniform blouse.

"You're as bad as your father," Gulan said.

Sarya smiled brightly, just as Daria jogged to them.

"The men from the next training camp want to play a game during their visit," Daria said.

"What sort of game?" Dila asked.

"Football or volleyball."

"Play volleyball," Sarya suggested while she looked towards about 20, mostly young men; just arrived near the gate. "Football involves a lot of running and that gives men an advantage."

"If you play volleyball, put Sarya in your team," Gulan said.

"Why?" Daria asked.

"You'll see."

"Put Gulan in your team too," Sarya said.

"Alright," Daria said, while looking unconvinced.

"Proper rules," Sarya said. "Six players a side; toss a coin to serve, a point on an error and that team serves, to twenty-five points." Sarya thought about that. "Let's take turns for serving within each team though."

Daria looked really confused about all that, before she ran to the men.

"Why do you want to rotate the serve?" Gulan asked.

"It's a friendly game," Sarya said.

The men chose six players while Sarya and Gulan joined Daria, Bemal, Vejan and Tara. The men tossed; Daria

120

called and lost. They gathered each side of a net strung between two houses, where a young man served for Gulan to intercept that; bouncing the ball high to Sarya, who jumped to hit that ball hard with her wrists, right through the men. There were a few profanities about the speed of that return, while the ball was retrieved for Gulan to serve.

Sarya let them bounce the ball back and forward for a while, before jumping and hitting it hard to score another point. That sequence went on, with the girls each taking turns to serve, a bit of a rally, and then Gulan intercepting the ball for Sarya to score the point. At Sarya's serve it was five-zero and she served fairly quickly; so the receiver couldn't control his return and bounced the ball towards the gate. And so it went on, with the women getting ever more excited while the men grew ever more despondent. The points kept on growing, and eventually the women won 25 to 0.

The winning team gathered in an impromptu circle of excitement, while six men wandered around looking as lost by as much as they'd just lost by.

"I didn't know you would be like that," Daria exclaimed.

"Like what?" Sarya asked innocently.

"Like that!"

"Don't ever get on the wrong end of Sarya's AK47," Gulan said, and then laughed.

"Let's not be bad winners," Sarya said; breaking away from the circle. She went to the men to shake their hands in commiseration, which they only begrudgingly accepted. All members of both teams eventually shook each other's hands.

"We've cooked a meal for our guests," Daria then announced, and that was a good time for lunch too. Daria escorted their guests to the large house where a feast had been laid out, after much effort by many helpers. That brightened the mood somewhat, and there were many happy conversations while eating.

"My name's Axa," the young man said.

"I'm Sarya," she said.

"Where did you learn to play like that?"

"Gulan and I played for our school team. I was captain."

"Oh. Do you like being in the YPJ?"

"Do you like being in the YPG?"

"I do, yes."

He was a nice boy and Sarya thought she could like him. She knew she was an age and she was curious, and another part of her was more than curious, especially when she had a nice boy to talk with. But that wasn't allowed. Normally that wasn't allowed anyway, but that didn't always prevent things. But in the YPG and the YPJ that definitely wasn't allowed and they'd agreed to that, so Sarya had to stand by that.

Komutan Rosnan sat next to Sarya too, and took some bread.

"Do you always play like that?" she asked.

"I usually play tougher," Sarya said. "But it was just a friendly game."

Rosnan laughed. "That was a good win by women over men," she said proudly.

Indeed it was.

* * *

The girls ran from building to building while pretending DAESH were there. Once they reached each building they ran from room to room and onto rooves too, before securing each building and moving to the next. Sarya stood back and watched with her rifle at the ready, but something didn't seem right. That seemed more like a game than war.

"What is it, Havel Sarya?" Komutan Rosnan asked.

"This doesn't seem right," Sarya said. "There could be DAESH terrorists here, but we know DAESH isn't in this village."

"Do you have an idea?"

Sarya looked across at her comrades. "One of us wears a dark windcheater," Sarya said. "She'll be a DAESH terrorist." A shot echoed. "We must be careful about the safeties on our rifles so we don't shoot each other."

"You have a dark windcheater so you can be DAESH."

The girls secured the village before reporting to Komutan Rosnan, who gave them new orders. Sarya went to her mattress where she discarded her flak jacket and pulled on her windcheater, although that summer's day was far too hot for such clothing. She went to the far side of the village and picked a house at random. There she waited, while thinking about DAESH terrorists. They would take out as many comrades as they could, probably before committing suicide.

Sarya heard footsteps on the gritty concrete floor as someone slowly approached. Closer and closer. Closer still, until Sarya stepped through the doorway with rifle aimed, and ambushed Gulan.

"You're dead," Sarya said, before retreating to the rear of the house. Carefully she peered through the open doorway and saw nothing, so she went to the next house. Again she hid, and again footsteps approached. Sarya stepped through the doorway to ambush Razhan.

"You're dead," Sarya said, when she heard footsteps from the roof. She climbed the staircase to near the top, where she saw Vian looking over the edge.

Sarya aimed her rifle. "You're dead," she shouted, before advancing to the parapet to kneel and look down. The other girls secured the remaining houses, and all seemed fine until Sarya stood and shouted to Komutan Rosnan that she had this house with three casualties.

They re-grouped in the village square where Sarya was glad to get rid of her hot windcheater.

"That was a useful exercise," Komutan Rosnan said. "Havel Sarya killed three of us, although in reality we would have heard her first shot. But there could have been three DAESH terrorists in this village, and they could have killed three of us because we weren't careful enough. To be a martyr to our cause is an honour, but our prime responsibility is to destroy DAESH, and we need to be alive to do that."

Later that evening when it was nearly dark, Sarya patrolled the earth bank with Gulan below her at the gate. Sarya heard something, and immediately spun around to aim at Komutan Rosnan. She lowered her rifle as Rosnan approached.

"You're formidable when you have a rifle in your hand, Havel Sarya," Komutan Rosnan said.

Sarya nodded.

"You're a bit of a loner," Rosnan said. "Except with a few friends."

"We can't all be the same," Sarya said.

"That was a good idea for our training exercise."

Sarya pondered that. "My father's a school headmaster, and he's encouraged me to think for myself."

"When you're on the front, discuss your ideas with your commander. I'm sure you'll have much to offer our collective army."

Rosnan moved away down the earth bank. Sarya resumed her task of staring into near darkness for any signs of light, while Gulan guarded the gate.

The next morning they did a parade ground exercise for the last time, and very well too. Then they took their oaths on the YPJ flag, before Komutan Rosnan read where they were being sent. Sarya felt sad that this group of farmer's daughters, little town merchant daughters, and daughters from the city, were to be sent to many different places. The names and destinations were read out, with those being sent together celebrating with each other. Then came Sarya Goran, Gulan Bashur, Dila Yasin and Medya Vali; all being sent to Hasakah. Gulan, Dila, Medya and Sarya all celebrated together. Sarya was more than pleased; she and her friends, who she persuaded to go to war, were being kept together.

There was time for one last song with 19 voices, before they boarded one of several Landcruisers waiting. It wasn't far to an abandoned village of about 100 houses not far from Hasakah; again protected by an earth bank and a sentry at a gate. It had a sign, Martyr Diyako, and the young man's picture.

There they were separated a second time. Gulan was sent to supplies, Dila was to be working with armaments, and Medya was to be a trained to be a sniper. Sarya was taken to a team of one woman and four men, who all stood when Sarya approached. There Sarya was introduced to Komutan

126

Mina, Havel Barî, Havel Keya, Havel Olan, and Havel Agir. Mina kissed Sarya three times, and welcomed her to their team.

Sarya was dumbfounded. She always assumed that to join the YPJ meant fighting DAESH, but of course that wasn't the case. There were many jobs in an army, and not all comrades fought on the front line. But she and Medya were two who would.

"Sarya," Mina said. "You've just been trained but there's still much for you to learn. We'll teach you the tricks to staying alive, and the tricks to defeating DAESH. In the meantime, can you tell us about yourself?"

Sarya did, while contemplating her team members. Mina was in her late thirties, taller than most women and as tall as Sarya, and she wore a black and purple headscarf. Mina had nice dimples when she smiled, which she did often. Keya was older and quite tall, and he had a beard. Barî was in his late twenties with a closely-cropped beard, and he had a camouflage cap which matched their uniforms. Agir was around the same age as Barî, but with a moustache rather than a beard. Barî looked a serious man, while Agir had a nice smile. Olan was fresh-faced young, perhaps Sarya's age, and tall and lanky. Olan looked out of place, while Sarya guessed she looked out of place as well.

"Now Sarya," Mina said. "As the newest member of our team, you can cook dinner for us. Olan will show you where the kitchen is."

Olan and Sarya walked across Camp Martyr Diyako. While they walked, Sarya realised that during training they took turns in cooking, and the men from the YPG would have done the same. That would have been something.

"Do you like cooking?" Sarya asked mischievously.

Olan shook his head. "No, no," he said emphatically.

"How was cooking during your training?"

"Awful! I never realised that cooking was so hard. We all take turns in our team; Mina included."

They reached a house where a temporary kitchen had bags of ingredients against a wall, more ingredients on a bench, piles of paper plates, many tea glasses, battered aluminium bowls and cauldrons; bottles of water in a vat of ice, and a couple of gas burners on the floor. A cauldron of tea stewed on one of those burners.

"Do you have any recommendations?" Sarya asked.

"You must be a better cook than me," Olan said.

Sarya looked at what she had available. "Don't expect miracles from what I have here," she said while checking the beef was alright. It was quite fresh, so Sarya poured a little oil into one of the pots, and chopped enough beef for six people. "I'll make beef stew with some rice," she said, while she set to cooking. "How long have you been part of this team?" Sarya asked.

"Two weeks," Olan said.

New like her. "Where are you from?"

"Afrin."

"From the city like me?"

"Yes."

Sarya opened a tin of tomatoes, a tin of string beans, and added enough water for consistently, and then let that stew while she dealt with the rice. There she had rice, salt, and a plastic bottle of lemon juice. That was set to cook as well.

"I'll fetch the others," Olan said.

Some time later they were sitting in a circle in the open, on a cool, August evening. Beef stew, rice and bread on paper plates, with a glass of tea each.

"This is good," Mina said. "There's a battle coming up soon, but I don't know where. In the meantime we wait."

Sarya understood, and that would give her a chance to better know her team. It would give her a chance to do some other things like wash her uniform, and she didn't know how to manage that with only one uniform to wear. They ate; they talked; while some teams played volleyball. All things would happen in good order, while they waited for the battle to come.

Chapter Twelve

Camp Martyr Diyako was an abandoned village of about 100 houses, around seven kilometres south of Hasakah. It was already buzzing with activity when Vache and Erna were driven inside the camp, protected by an earth bank bulldozed into place, except for a gap as the entry road, with a gate and a sentry on duty. Inside was a near-grid of paved streets mostly lined by modest houses built of concrete block; all painted white, and all with flat rooves. Near the centre of the village was a garage workshop or something of that sort. Vache commandeered that for their surgery, and he commandeered the house next door, for the doctor, Erna the qualified nurse, and for the unqualified nurses the tabûr would assign to them in time. The workshop was a good size and would allow treatment of a few patients at a time. Vache got the house in order with a couple of mattresses, a couple of chairs, and curtains across a room doorway and across the window for privacy. With that, a gas burner and a cauldron, they had all the comforts of home. Erna readied the surgery, where Vache was pleased to see an examination table, a small table for implements, four chairs, and their medical equipment being stowed on shelves assembled along one wall.

"Do you want a coffee?" Vache asked.

"Yes please," Erna responded.

He made two mugs and brought them to the surgery, and they relaxed while suppliers and armourers were busy in two houses nearby.

"Something's going to happen soon," Erna said, while she watched the activity.

"I would say they're taking villages to the south of here, with the eventual aim of taking al-Shaddadah," Vache said. "Al-Shaddadah's the major stronghold for DAESH in this part of Syria."

"That'll be easier said than done."

That was true. Syria had villages every few kilometres, with probably 200 or more villages between Hasakah and al-Shaddadah. The tabûr consisted of about 300 front-line troops, broken into teams of anything from six men and women to 10 or even 15. This camp was home for one tabûr and about 40 teams, plus support personnel.

"Have you heard the news?" Erna asked.

Vache hadn't heard anything in particular. "Go on, tell me," he said. "I'm dying of suspense."

"Today's the formation of the Syrian Democratic Forces. They've joined the YPG and the YPJ with some Arab defence militias, a Turkmen militia, and the Syriac Military Council. Obviously under pressure from the Western Coalition, they've moved from a Kurdish army, to a Kurdish-dominated, multi-ethnic army."

"I admire their pragmatism," Vache said.

"Me too. They're great fighters, no, they're natural-born fighters, they've achieved women's equality that far exceeds anything done in the West, they've gotten the West onside through their great military achievements, and now they compromise to keep the West supporting them. DAESH doesn't stand a chance.'

"As they take al-Shaddadah and other cities, it's no longer Kurds taking Arab land, but rather a coalition including Arabs and even Christians."

"Much more palatable all round."

Vache watched Kurds cheerfully readying their camp, as they were always cheerful. For sure, DAESH didn't stand a chance.

* * *

Sarya picked her way through the house; watching for IEDs and trip wires while she held her rifle ready to deal with any terrorists who crossed her path. From the opposite direction Olan did the same, but unfortunately he missed a tip wire. For a young man he swore colourfully.

Sarya jogged up the stairs to the roof, used for sleeping on hot nights, while missing booby traps on the way. She made it through Barî's test intact and ready to deal with a terrorist. She went downstairs and outside.

"Well done," Barî said, and that made Sarya feel proud. Compliments didn't flow easy from her teammate.

"You'll have to do better, Olan," Barî said. "One IED and you're dead."

Olan nodded.

"Enough of that," Agir said. 'Mina's prepared lunch and that's more important!"

That sat in the shade of the house doubling as kitchen, and ate Mina's lunch of fish with rice and bread, washed down with tea.

"We've been challenged," Mina said. "Question is: volleyball or football?"

"Volleyball," Sarya said. "I was team captain."

"Anyone else?" Mina asked.

They didn't have preferences either way, so volleyball it was, against Komutan Hedar's team.

The game started off casually with friendly banter whenever someone made a simple mistake, but got ever more serious once the stakes were realised. There were no stakes but honour, and that was important. Sarya watched their team lose a few points, before she decided to help things along. From then on they didn't lose a point, all the way to victory. There was much cheering and commiserations, although fake commiserations. Clearly the best team won.

They celebrated with an afternoon cup of tea, while Mina went to a tabûr briefing. Sarya knew she was young and inexperienced, but what surprised her was how much they took her into their hearts and made her feel an important part of their team. She was glad she could reward their comradeship by helping their game of volleyball.

"When you said you were team captain, you weren't joking," Agir said.

"I'm taller than most girls my age, and that helps," Sarya said.

"That and an aggressive style. Half as good as that on the battlefield and you'll be alright."

"War's different I'm sure," Sarya said.

He lightly punched her arm in a friendly, supportive way. "We're not so old that we don't remember what it's like to first go to war."

"Thank you."

Mina sat in their circle. "Tomorrow we start the al-Hawl Offensive," she said. "There are over 200 villages between here and al-Shaddadah, and we've been assigned villages in groups of one to three teams, depending on village size and expected resistance. As always DAESH terrorists will be dug-in, so we have to flush them out. We'll use airstrikes, and then go in on foot. They think there're about a thousand DAESH terrorists to deal with, but they may bring in more. We'll have a good meal this evening, get an early night's sleep, and be ready first thing in the morning."

There was silence and Sarya felt a little sick to her stomach. Keya then stood and sang the first line of Ey Dijmin, the Kurdish national anthem, and they all stood and

134

sang with him. Sarya felt her eyes water while she sang. She loved her country, she loved her people, and she loved these men and Mina. For sure the Kurdish youth were ready and prepared to give their lives as the supreme sacrifice. Sarya was proud to be a part of this, and she knew she would do her duty when the time came for it.

* * *

Early dawn on the last day of October 2015, and Camp Martyr Diyako just outside Hasakah bustled with activity. Men and women climbed into the backs of utilities and vans, all talking noisily and clearly excited about the battle to come. Some singing patriotic songs while they squeezed into vehicles. Mina's team climbed into the rear of a Toyota utility, with Sarya waiting for the men to sort themselves out. They were talking cheerfully but Sarya felt sick to her stomach. Beside her, Olan was confronting his first battle too. They climbed on last, to sit on the sides of the tray and face each other while the driver slammed the tailgate shut.

Olan leaned forward. "I'll protect you," he said seriously.

Sarya was amused his sincerity and smiled brightly at that. "You mean I'll protect you," she said.

The Toyota lurched away to join a convoy of six teams to take three villages, plus three Technicals: utilities fitted with large calibre machine guns on the tray. The buzz of excitement became infectious after a time, and Sarya's sickness faded. They sang Golnar Kurmanji and Sarya couldn't help but sing along. Not Olan who looked really sombre. From high in the sky Sarya looked down on a utility, where she saw a 19 year old girl in a green camouflage uniform, a green headscarf for her femininity, with an AK47 between her knees, singing with grizzled veterans of many battles. Some of those men and Mina had turned the DAESH advance on Kobanî around, and took what seemed like inevitable defeat into a series of victories, pushing ever closer to the city of al-Shaddadah. To be amongst those men and women seemed strangely surreal.

On a cloudy and slightly misty morning, utilities dropped two teams about a rifle shot short of a large, white barn, with the village further beyond that. Men and women from those teams jumped down and immediately ran to that barn. Sarya joined them in the sprint across a field green with a crop of some sort, while some shot their rifles towards the village. The teams reached the barn and gathered together.

"Barî and Agir cover me while I check," Mina said.

Barî moved from behind the barn to fire towards the village, with many shots fired in reply by DAESH while Mina stood behind him. Barî was replaced by Agir while Mina continued to scan. Mina returned to safety behind the barn to study her tablet computer and converse with the Komutan Hedar. Mina reached for her scrambled radio to request an airstrike. A distorted voice acknowledged her request.

There they waited, until a Coalition jet closed from a distance; closer and closer until it swooped over the village and climbed steeply away. A massive explosion followed, and all that could be heard was an aircraft returning to its carrier.

"Now we go," Mina said.

Again they sprinted across a field of green vegetables. Sarya had her rifle ready, when suddenly rifle shots crackled from the village. Men and women stopped to shoot at the village, so Sarya paused, aimed and shot a few rounds in the general direction of the village too, before running once more. The field echoed with shots from DAESH in the village and shots from men and women closing. Sarya ran hard to a white wall around a two-storey building. She pressed herself against that wall with Keya and Barî.

A shot hit the wall immediately above their heads, and they'd been targeted by a DAESH sniper! Another shot crackled into the wall with brick dust falling into Sarya's hair. For sure they'd been targeted by a patient sniper. Keya and Barî looked past the wall while shooting at the village, in an attempt to locate that second DAESH position.

Still the shots crackled in, with the DAESH sniper not able to hit them but trapping them against that wall. Sarya moved to the other end of the wall for a better view; before shooting towards the village like Keya and Barî, to locate the sniper. Suddenly she sensed something and ducked, to see a rocket flash past where she'd been standing, to explode somewhere beyond. Sarya looked up in shock. That was close! She drew a deep breath to calm herself before resuming her surveillance, and there was one likely house. Sarya sensed someone alongside, and moved to be with Mina.

"Second on the left is a house where I think the sniper is," Sarya said.

"Cover me while I check," Mina said.

Mina peered around the corner while Sarya stood above her and shot towards the sniper, and immediately a shot hit the wall above their heads. That was positive proof.

Mina pulled back and radioed the crew of the technical, who rolled into position and opened fire with their large calibre machine gun. They shot at that house while Mina conferred with Hedar. He offered to take that house, while Mina would advance on the ruined house and deal with any DEASH who may have survived the airstrike.

Sarya and Mina returned to the rest of their team at the far right of the wall. There Barî tapped Sarya on the shoulder, and immediately they ran across gravelly ground as a group. They reached the ruined house and went from room to room over rubble, rifles at the ready, but there was nothing but two dead DAESH terrorists.

Shots crackled from yet another house, and Mina knelt to look through a window without glass.

Barî and Agir and we'll cover," Mina said, while she got her rifle ready.

The two men ran to that house, with the rest of their team firing towards that house but away from their comrades. Sarya watched her comrades press against the wall.

Sarya and Keya, and we'll cover," Mina said.

Sarya followed Keya, and moments later she was pressed against a white painted wall. Barî told Sarya to climb the outside stairs to the roof, Keya to the back while he and Agir went inside.

Head down, Sarya jogged part-way up the staircase, while watching out for trip-wires and IEDs. She paused when she reached the parapet at the top, to see the DAESH terrorist who'd been shooting at her comrades. Sarya climbed another step to aim and then shoot at the terrorist, before ducking her head as a volley of bullets hurtled in her direction. Again she put her head up to aim and shoot at him, and like slow-motion he dropped his rifle with a clatter and fell backwards while clutching his right shoulder. *Now what should she do?* Sarya climbed onto the roof with her rifle trained on the young, bearded terrorist, who scrabbled away with his eyes full of fear. Maybe he was frightened of dying, or maybe if a woman killed him, he would go to hell. Sarya steadily closed when he reached for a cord hanging by his waist. Sarya knew what that was, and spun around to protect herself when the explosion boomed with a rush of hot air.

Heart beating ever faster, Sarya turned back to see body parts strewn all over the roof. Arm here, leg there, foot somewhere else. Even his hair and scalp was blown from his head. She felt dampness on her hair and realised she'd been showered with his remains.

Sarya fought bile rising in her throat to go to the parapet, where she saw a figure in black running towards this house. She aimed and shot, but the terrorist kept on running.

Sarya ran down those stairs and entered the house, to spot a family cowering in the corner. The terrorist came into sight just as Keya shot from one side, and the terrorist crumpled to his knees.

"Good work," Barî said to Keya.

"There was a DAESH terrorist on the roof, but he blew himself up," Sarya said.

"He didn't want to be killed by a woman," Barî said. "Agir; look after this one and keep this house secure. Keya and Sarya come with me."

They ran to the next house and pressed against the wall. Sarya followed Barî inside, and with rifle carefully trained she went from room to room; looking out for booby traps and searching for DAESH. Keya sprinted up an internal staircase to the roof. All around the village, shots crackled and crackled again.

House clear and empty; they then ran to the next house and that was clear. After what seemed like just minutes, but was undoubtable longer, they reached the last house and were confronted with more green fields. More and more SDF[4] gathered beyond that village, the shooting faded to silence, and Mina came with the rest of their team, except Agir guarding their prisoner.

They stood in a circle.

"Let me know what happened," Mina asked.

"I wounded a terrorist and Agir has him," Keya said.

Mina nodded. "Olan," she said. "Find Agir and take that prisoner to the ambulances.

Olan headed off.

"We'll patch him up if we can," Mina said. "He'll end up in Rojava, and probably be traded."

Sarya understood.

"Anything else?" Mina asked.

"A terrorist blew himself up after I wounded him," Sarya said.

"He didn't want to be killed by a woman. We've taken this village and saved a few human shields, so this was a good morning's work. Do you have any comments, Sarya?"

Sarya paused to gather her thoughts. "This wasn't what I expected," she said. "I wouldn't have managed without the extra training you gave us."

---

[4] SDF – Syrian Democratic Forces

"Thank you Sarya." Mina said. "Congratulations to all of you for a job well done. As you know, now we wait. Rations, water, and we secure this village."

Sarya felt really, really exhausted. She didn't know how long it was, perhaps two or three hours, but she was as drained as if that battle lasted all day. The men and Mina too. Lifelessly they sat on the ground, leaned against the wall of a house; holding their rifles while they smoked and stared into the distance. Sarya sat with them; glad it was over and glad she'd survived.

But it wasn't over; they had to secure that village until nearby villages were taken by the SDF. When DAESH was driven from the near vicinity, they could move on. In the meantime, the people who called that village home would return when they heard the news. Mina conferred with Hedar, where Hedar agreed to do the first patrol. Four men and two woman, working in pairs, scanned for any movement on the plain. The rest were free to relax and recover for a time.

* * *

A white van drove up, the driver opened the rear doors, and a comrade jumped down to unpack bottled water in plastic wrap; several bottles wrapped together. They dropped white plastic shopping bags onto the ground, but one big bag attracted the most attention. A bag of Arden cigarette cartons, where most exchanged money for packs of cigarettes, Olan included. The other bags contained tinned food and cartons of cheese. Sarya helped herself to one of each, and a bottle of water, before sitting. Olan sat beside her.

"You're too young to be smoking that," Sarya said. "Do you even know how?"

"I'm old enough," he said defensively.

She punched his arm. "I was joking." She opened the tin to prod the contents with her spoon. "What's this?"

"Chicken," Mina said flatly.

Sarya prodded the thick goo while her stomach heaved, and she wondered why she felt sick. She put the tin aside and pondered the cheese instead. A triangle of soft cheese wrapped in silver paper, with a label which had a picture of a cow. Still Sarya's stomach heaved and she knew why. She couldn't get away from thoughts of that terrorist spread from one end of the roof to the other. He was a DAESH terrorist and her enemy, but that was truly awful. Instead Sarya drank some water while the buzz of conversations got ever louder. They needed food, even tinned chicken with strange cheese, to revive their spirits. Or they needed those cigarettes.

Agir, Barî and Keya got up to arrange themselves in a line, while Sarya watched them. Soon they were singing and dancing.

"Come on Mina," Sarya said, and her commander joined Sarya in the line of men. Sarya beckoned Olan and he took her hand to join the dance. They sang and danced until nearly exhausted; where dancing was replaced by happy conversations with more smoking and more bottles of water. They stood in groups while Sarya sat with Mina to have quality, girl time together.

"When you trained," Sarya said. "Did you dance?"

"A lot," Mina said with a bright smile."

"I like men, but there's nothing like twenty women's voices."

Mina smiled brightly, and Sarya knew she'd revived good memories from a long time ago.

"I love this," Sarya said for no reason she could think of.

"I know what you mean," Mina said.

"I love you all," Sarya said, while unable to explain that. Then it came to her. "You're my family," she said.

"You're my family, and I look after you all."

"Like an older sister."

"Yes," Mina said.

Sarya gazed across the lush farmland. "This is a beautiful place, and one day there'll be peace here."

Mina looked peculiar. She was pale and yet flushed, and holding her mouth in a funny way.

"I think there was something wrong with my chicken," she said, before jumping up and running to the village. The men broke into big laughter.

"Did you put something in her food?" Sarya asked.

"No; the food's bad enough to do that," Agir replied while smiling brightly.

Sarya didn't think that was funny at all. Mina returned, sat, drank some water, stood, and ran off again. Again the men laughed, and this time Sarya couldn't help herself.

"You're all bad influences!" she exclaimed.

"This looks like a happy team," a voice commented.

Sarya looked up to see a comrade with two other men: both wearing camouflage and body armour, but not SDF. One held a big video camera while the other must have been a reporter.

"I'm looking for Komutan Mina," the comrade asked.

The men laughed again, while Sarya struggled to keep a straight face.

"Komutan Mina is in the village," Sarya said mischievously.

The soldier and the two men headed towards the village.

"You can't go there!" Olan exclaimed.

"Why not?" the comrade asked.

"Um.....'

Sarya guessed what these men wanted, from the YouTube clips she saw. "You want a woman's version of our victory today," she said.

That was his turn for 'um'.

145

"You want to film something on the YPJ," Sarya clarified.

"Yes we do."

Sarya felt it wasn't appropriate to commentate like she was a commander, but she could do something else. "How about we re-enact part of the battle, with me?"

"We could do that."

"Are you all, alright with this?" Sarya asked the team.

"It's been a long day," Barî grumbled.

"We'll be famous on YouTube."

"What's YouTube?"

"You don't know YouTube? We'll be actors on the internet."

"Come on Barî," Olan said. "We can do this without you."

"Alright," he said, not too convincingly. "How do we do this?"

Sarya thought. "We'll go to the ruined house and shoot like there are terrorists. Then we'll run to the next house still shooting."

"That's all?"

"That's all."

"Alright," he said; getting to his feet with rifle in hand. They trooped to the bombed house, followed by the comrade with the two men. Sarya took charge, and on her lead they waged war on an empty house, taking turns, with Sarya taking

146

a few turns because she knew that's what the SDF really wanted. Then Sarya told them to take that empty house, before she led the way across and inside. There the shooting abated.

Sarya went outside to the comrade. "Was that alright?" she asked.

The comrade asked the film crew in English, and they said it was good.

"I'm glad we could help," Sarya said in English.

"You speak English?" the reporter asked.

"I do."

The reporter shook hands with her. "Thank you so much," he said.

"That was our pleasure. Now, we must go back and secure this village."

They left.

"What was it you said?" Keya asked in Kurdish.

"I told them we have to secure the village," Sarya said.

"Yes we do. Let's go."

They went to the far side of the village, where Mina waited. "What was that shooting?" she asked.

"A film crew wanted to film us," Keya said.

"Oh."

"We put on a mock battle for them" Sarya said.

"It's a pity I missed out."

Then Mina looked funny and ran off again. Sarya hoped that never happened to her.

Mina returned a short while later and sat amongst them. She looked across the lush, green crop. "This is a beautiful country, spoiled by war," she said.

It was.

Sarya contemplated the vast, open plain once more. She loved this country and she loved her people. More, she loved her team; the grizzled veterans of many battles. She loved them enough to lay her life down for them.

Chapter Thirteen

The village of al-Khamail was a bleak and featureless huddle of about 100 houses just off the highway, and also well defended by DAESH.

Like last time they were dropped relatively close to the village, and from there they ran to a large, partly ruined house beyond the outskirts, where they took refuge behind a wall near a green, slimy swimming pool. There Mina took stock of the situation, studied her tablet computer; discussed the situation with Komutan Hedar, before calling for an airstrike. They waited, until a Coalition warplane roared in to obliterate hopefully the only house with DAESH. Mina then instructed Barî and Agir to check that ruined house, while the rest provided cover. In the meantime, Hedar had his team advancing to the left.

Sarya watched Barî and Agir run across open ground and through what was once the front door. Moments later they gave the all clear. Their team moved to that house.

"The next house should be clear," Mina said. "Agir and Sarya check it out, and we'll cover you."

Agir went to the back door of the ruined house and paused, before sprinting across open ground with Sarya following, while the others provided cover. Agir then Sarya reached the front door of the next house and went inside. As always Sarya was alert for IEDs, human shields and DAESH.

Once ground floor rooms were searched, it was time to climb to the roof. All clear, so Agir beckoned the rest of their team across.

Shooting echoed across the village from the other team. Mina asked Agir and Sarya to check the next house along; again while being covered. They did that, and after a few minutes of searching, all was clear. In the background, above the noise of rifles and machine guns, Sarya swore she heard an engine screaming. Agir must have heard it because he went to the back door. Sarya followed to where she saw the strangest car: all box-like and finished in grey steel plate, and even with wheels and tyres shielded by steel. The suicide car rolled past, but clearly the driver peering through his tiny window had another target. Agir must have realised this and he ran to a gathering of comrades near a bigger building, with their backs to imminent danger.

Suddenly the earth shook with a massive explosion, and the suicide car was engulfed by a huge fireball 20 or even 30 metres in size. Sarya felt a sharp pain to her head, and dropped her rifle in shock. She went to pick it up, while warm wetness ran down the side of her nose. She grabbed her rifle only to topple, and everything felt heavy and furry. She tried to stand but couldn't. Her legs were useless while she felt so tired. Sarya felt very, very tired.

* * *

Sarya was sitting in a room with something thick around her head. She wondered where she was and how she got there. Ahead, two men in dark clothes talked quietly in Arabic while they looked through a window without glass. Beside her was a mattress, which had a woman in a black abaya who had her face uncovered. Sarya looked around that room and saw several IEDs made from plastic bottles beyond that mattress; near her flak jacket and her rifle propped against the wall. She'd been captured by DAESH, and gradually things came clear. She was hit by something when the suicide car blew-up, and they captured her. Why? To trade her, execute her, or sexually abuse her? Sarya looked at the woman in black and their eyes met, and to Sarya they seemed like friendly eyes. Was that woman a DAESH bride; someone who'd voluntarily joined their cause, or was she a sex slave? Sarya contemplated her options. She could creep past this woman and grab her rifle from beyond, and shoot those men. Slowly, Sarya made to move from where she sat, but she felt dizzy and almost fell. Sarya paused, before trying again, and again she almost fell. For some reason she couldn't move. Could she do it from where she sat? Possibly.

Then the man on the right spoke into a radio where a scratchy and distorted voice responded, and that noise and distraction would work. Sarya glanced at that woman while wondering if she could trust her. Sarya realised her situation couldn't be any worse. Sarya looked at the woman while putting her finger over lips. The woman nodded. Sarya pointed at her rifle and then at herself, but the woman looked frightened and shook her head. A second time Sarya pointed at her rifle and then at herself, but the woman looked blank. Sarya mouthed 'please' in Arabic, and the woman nodded her head.

Sarya watched the woman ease herself off the mattress, and on hands and knees reach for the rifle, before slowly, carefully, bringing it to the mattress. Sarya glanced at the two men engrossed in their radio conversation about another suicide car for the battle, before she took her rifle in her hands. With the radio squawking loudly, Sarya braced her right shoulder against the wall, raised her rifle, nudged the safety, sharply slid the bolt; quickly aimed and squeezed the trigger three times.

As always the shots were deafening in a confined space, and so close she couldn't miss. He fell to the floor. Sarya immediately aimed at the man on the right who turned his head with his mouth open wide, and she squeezed the trigger three times. He fell to the floor where two sets of black clothes turned red, and blood ran across a concrete floor.

Sarya locked the safety and leaned her head against the wall in quiet contemplation. She turned her head to face the woman.

"Who are you?" Sarya asked in Arabic.

152

"My name's Leila Khider," she said. "I'm Yazidi."

Sarya was surprised. "Do you speak Kurmanji Kurdish?" she asked.

"I do," Leila said in Kurdish

"My name's Sarya Goran of the SDF," Sarya said in Kurdish.

"Are those men dead?"

"Yes." Sarya went to move and felt dizzy, but less so. "Can you help me to stand?"

Leila did just that. Standing, Sarya felt somewhat better.

"Can you get that strange jacket for me?" Sarya asked.

Leila handed over the flak jacket, and Sarya slipped it on.

"We'll go outside to find help," Sarya said.

Leila helped Sarya to the ground floor of a two-storey house, and outside to where her comrades seemed to have the upper hand. Sarya got her bearings on the drop-off point where ambulances waited. But there was one thing first. She saw Havel Nefel nearby.

"Nefel," she said. "I overheard DAESH ordering another suicide car."

Nefel's eyes grew big with shock. "Thank you Sarya," she said, before sprinting away, no doubt to one of the commanders. Sarya hoped they could blow-up that suicide car with an anti-tank missile, while she directed Leila out of the village to where two white vans waited, with drivers conversing and smoking. As Sarya closed, a driver butted his cigarette and came to her.

"What happened to you?" he asked.

"I was hit by shrapnel from the suicide car," Sarya said. "This woman helped me."

"Your bandage is wet with blood."

Sarya touched her forehead and indeed it was.

"Both of you climb in the back," the driver said.

They did, doors were slammed closed, and they were on their way.

Sarya sat on a stretcher, opposite a rack holding medical equipment. Leila sat beside her.

"Thank you for rescuing me," Leila said.

"Thank you for helping me back there," Sarya said. "Did those men carry me in?"

"They did."

"Where are you from?"

"I'm from Sinjar. More than a year ago, DAESH attacked us even though we were unarmed. They took many young women and killed everyone else. My whole family's dead: mother, father and younger brother. I was taken close to here by bus with other women, where they put us in a pen. Then I was given to a DAESH man for a time, until he sold me to the man you killed."

Sarya was shocked. "I'm sorry for your losses," she said, while knowing that wasn't enough. She looked Leila in the eyes. "I'm truly devastated by your losses."

Leila put her head down. "You're destroying DAESH and that's more important. You're risking your life to rid the earth of these barbarians."

Sarya nodded her head slowly in agreement. She'd heard stories about Yazidi sex slaves, but to be face-to-face with such brutality was a different experience. Family murdered; a young woman taken and raped multiple times, and when the terrorist tired of her or wanted a fresh victim, he sold her like cattle.

Suddenly the van swerved onto rough ground and Sarya grabbed for the rack opposite to stop from falling. She heard another vehicle, and then a burst of heavy machine gun fire. Gan! They'd been targeted by a DAESH Technical!

"Keep low," Sarya said, while she flattened herself on the mattress. Leila lay beside Sarya who held her tight. The van accelerated while weaving left and right, under fire from the machine gun. On and on they sped, when a round ripped through the side of the van; punching holes in the metalwork above them. For the first time, Sarya felt she was going to die. They were alone on the plain under attack, with no means of defence. The engine revved; the driver did his best, and they swerved off roughness onto what must have been the bitumen road again. Really speeding now with everything

155

shaking in the rear. Another burst from behind which missed. And then silence, apart from the abused engine. They sped for a time before slowing, and then resumed a cruise. All seemed safe. Sarya sat up and Leila sat up as well.

"We got away," the driver said.

"Thank you for your good driving," Sarya said.

He turned around and grinned, and Sarya couldn't help but smile back. He'd done well and he was proud of that, and in war nothing was more important than a job done well.

They slowed, and through the front window of the ambulance, Sarya saw Camp Martyr Diyako. They passed the gate, and moments later the van eased to a halt, the engine died, and rear doors opened. The driver looked at the holes in the sides and whistled with a big smile.

"That was close," Sarya said.

He nodded, before helping her down. Sarya felt just a little dizzy while he led her into a building; open at the front like a garage for cars. To the right, shelves were stocked with medical equipment, while there was a wooden bed, a wooden table which was covered with medical items, and a few plastic chairs further away. A tall man with fair skin was cutting at stiches on a long scratch on a young comrade lying on the bed. A woman with medium-length, dark hair moved in and wiped antiseptic over that scratch. The doctor tapped the comrade on the back and told him in Arabic that he would be fine. The comrade climbed down while fastening his shirt buttons. The tall man then turned to Sarya and shook her hand.

"I'm Vache," he said in Arabic in a deep, deep voice.

"I'm Sarya," she replied in Arabic. "A suicide car blew up and I was knocked unconscious by shrapnel. I was very dizzy for a time, but I'm feeling just a little dizzy now."

He nodded. "Please sit on the bed."

Sarya rested her rifle to one side before she sat. Vache took a small torch from his pocket and shined it in her eyes while looking intently.

"Follow my finger," he said, while moving forward, backward, left and right.

"You've been concussed, and you may feel dizzy and disorientated on and off for the next few days. Rest here for three days, and then see me so I can test you again. Now, let's look at that bandage."

He unwrapped the thick, cotton bandage around Sarya's forehead.

"Who bandaged you?" he asked.

"DAESH," Sarya said.

"Really?"

"They captured me but I escaped."

He looked at her forehead and frowned. "I'll stitch this wound," he said. "Erna," he said.

The woman came with a bottle and a cotton ball.
"This will sting," she said in Arabic, while she wiped Sarya's
cut with antiseptic. In the meantime, Vache tore open a
paper pouch and pulled out a needle with thread.

"This is like sewing," Sarya said.

"Indeed it is," Vache replied.

Sarya was surprised by this man's abilities. "Are you a
doctor?" she asked.

"I'm a doctor and Erna's a nurse."

He sewed Sarya's skin like sewing material, and it
didn't even hurt that much. He looped the thread around and
around before cutting it.

"Come back in about five days for Erna or I to
remove these stitches."

Sarya nodded. "Thank you Vache."

He nodded. "Don't forget to rest here for three days
and then get tested by me. It's important for you to rest
before you return to battle." He smiled. "Alright?"

"Alright Vache."

Sarya shook his hand, took her rifle, and left his
makeshift surgery. She'd never been to a doctor before,
because she'd never been sick, apart from the usual colds and
flu. And even though her injuries weren't so bad, that doctor
Vache had to deal with all sorts of terrible injuries. Soldiers
shot with bullets and many other injuries. But just the way he
tested her with his torch and then a finger. He must have so

much knowledge. Sarya was impressed. She'd always done well at school; well enough to go to university like Daran. She could become a doctor! That would help her people like Vache helped her wounded comrades.

Sarya wasn't hungry but she needed water. She went to the kitchen and introduced herself to the comrades there: drivers, suppliers and comrades of that sort. She propped her rifle against the wall, grabbed a bottle of water from the ice vat, and sat with them in their circle. They had a plate of cheeses and sausages. Perhaps she was hungry after all!

* * *

Vache boiled coffee on the gas hotplate, and then carefully poured two mugs. He gave one to Erna and sat in the chair beside her. He sipped while thinking about that young woman with a rifle. How old was she? Eighteen or nineteen? What was her name? Havel Sarya.

"What are you thinking about, my love?" Erna asked.

"That young woman with concussion," Vache said. "They're so young, and yet they fight battles with automatic rifles without a moment's hesitation. She was captured by DAESH and she escaped."

"Really?" Erna asked.

Vache sipped his coffee and nodded.

"Now that is something!" Erna exclaimed.

"I don't know what happens when this war is over and these people return to normal lives," Vache said. But what

159

they've got here, now, is something special. I see these women time and again, and every time it blows me away. We have feminism and what we think is equality, like you with your career, but what they have is something more deeply rooted."

"Their theory of jineology."

"Yes. Jineology has worked well in this war, and I truly hope it survives peace."

"The patriarchy has a reason for jineology not to survive, which is to retain male power, so we shall see."

Vache sipped his coffee while he contemplated that. Kurdish women were so remarkably capable that he truly hoped they had the chance to use their talents in peace after war.

Chapter Fourteen

Vache liked early mornings, and mornings were the only husband and wife time they had. One day war would be over and he would be left with memories of what they'd shared, including many mornings together. He lay on his side while admiring Erna's face in light filtered by a thin curtain.

Outside the camp stirred, and Vache slid out of bed to dress before lighting the gas. A short time later he sat on their bed with a mug of coffee, while Erna sat up to drink her mug. No matter how many times; he was always startled by her beauty. They finished drinking, where Erna dressed in slacks and a t-shirt. They went to the communal kitchen where there was fresh bread, honey, tea, and bottles of water. Young Sarya was there; spreading honey over bread.

"Marhaba Sarya," Vache said. "How do you feel?"

"Marhaba Vache," Sarya said. "I feel better than yesterday."

She sat on the floor cross-legged, with her bread and a glass of tea. Vache sat beside her and Erna sat opposite.

"You have no idea how much nicer this food is than what we have to eat," Sarya said.

Then make the most of it," Vache said.

"I will." She looked at him. "You're not Kurds."

"We're Armenian."

"Ah."

"Who would have thought that DAESH could unite so many different peoples against them?"

She smiled. "Who would have thought?" She drank some tea. "When we were trained, we were asked what we wanted to do after this war. Most wanted to be teachers, but I didn't know what I wanted. Now I want to be a doctor."

Vache was touched.

"To be a doctor," Erna said. "All you need to know is how to boss nurses around."

Sarya's mouth fell open.

Erna put her hand on Vache's hand. "We're married," she said.

"Husband and wife; doctor and nurse," Sarya said.

"That's right," Vache said. "To be a doctor is a four-year university degree, followed by a one-year internship in a hospital. Then two years supervised work experience before you can practice on your own."

"My brother's doing a four-year university course in law, so that's not so much different."

"No, it's not. There are two tricks to passing university. The first trick is they bury you in work like assignments, essays and practicals. To pass you need to set aside enough time for this work, and prioritise your workload so it's all done on time. If you can manage your workload you will pass. The second trick is writing everything down to memorise it. Lectures are just a lecturer talking, but you'll never remember what he says unless you write it down, in some sort of abbreviated way. When the time comes for exams, re-write your lecture notes and that will embed them in your memory."

"Thank you for that," Sarya said before sipping her tea.

"Do you speak English?"

"Yes I do."

"Many medical papers are in English, so that'll help. Also, you have the option of studying overseas in America or England, or other countries like Australia."

Sarya nodded her head. "And then return here to help my people."

"Yes," Vache said; touched by her authenticity.

She finished her bread and tea and stood. "Now I must rest."

She left them.

"She's so young and yet so mature," Erna said. "Her parents must be proud of her."

That went without saying.

* * *

Sarya dreamt of shouting and rifle fire. She woke with a start to realise that wasn't a dream. There was shouting and rifle fire! She jumped to her feet, grabbed her rifle, and raced to the gate, where several comrades were shooting from the top of the earth bank. She raced to the top to spot a grey truck in the distance. Like a suicide car, only bigger. An AK47 had no chance with steel plate, yet if that truck broke through the gate and detonated in the camp, then everyone would be killed.

Sarya raced down the bank hoping to find an anti-tank missile like they saw on the video during training, and better still, someone to shoot it. She ran to armaments, where she spotted Dila.

"Dila!" Sarya shouted. "Do we have an anti-tank missile launcher?"

"This one," Dila said. "An RPG-7."

"Do you know who can use it?"

"No."

Sarya was in a camp of drivers, suppliers, doctors, and nurses. She had as good a chance as anyone. "Grab a few missiles and come with me."

Sarya exchanged her rifle for the RPG, and ran past the gate to scale the bank, with Dila just behind. From the top she saw the grey truck, surely a chariot of death, lumbering across the plains. The road looped into the camp, so she had the side of the truck in view. The truck was about 150 metres away and just cruising, which gave her enough time for two shots. Sarya quickly familiarised herself with the handles, trigger and sights; before taking a missile from Dila and feeding it into the front of the launcher. Sarya lifted the RPG onto her shoulder, stood, and sighted the truck through the two sights; a lot like a rifle. She squeezed the trigger, and the missile launched with a boom and whoosh; with little recoil. Sarya watched the truck continue at the same, steady speed. She fed another missile, stood, and this time aimed by following the moving vehicle, before squeezing the trigger. Again a boom and whoosh, followed moments later by a massive explosion and fireball which continued along the road for 50 or 60 metres. Smoke cleared to reveal scorched bitumen and no sign of the truck at all. On the other side of the gate, comrades with rifles danced and cheered, before some realised an anti-tank missile saved the day.

Sarya felt dizzy and sat on the ground, while Dila looked across the plain with her mouth open. Then she knelt.

"You saved us," she said.

"We saved us, Dila," Sarya said. She stood and hugged her friend from school. "We make a good team," she said.

Dila hugged Sarya, and Sarya wished they could fight together. Then she felt dizzy and had to sit again.

"Are you alright?" Vache asked.

"I'm dizzy," Sarya said while looking up at the doctor.

"You should rest now. I'll help you."

Sarya stood where Vache held her arm, and led her down the bank towards a house.

"Do you want some coffee?" Vache asked.

"Coffee!" Sarya exclaimed. :"Where do you get coffee?"

"Just come with me."

Vache took Sarya into that house, past a curtain, and into a room with two mattresses pushed together. She sat on one of two plastic chairs. He lit a gas burner, and soon they had mugs of coffee each.

"It's not great coffee," Vache said. "But it is coffee."

"Any coffee's good coffee," Sarya said with a big smile.

Vache looked hard at her. "I think you saved us."

She shrugged her shoulders. "My commander trained us well, and maybe when you've been in battle you react differently."

"I forgive you for running about, but now you must rest."

"I will." She sipped her coffee. "Do you know if the woman I came with is still here?"

"Yes she is."

"I don't understand why men would do that to a woman."

"Their ideology is Islam as it was one-thousand, three-hundred years ago; when men had multiple wives and sex slaves."

"Islam doesn't do that anymore; except for DAESH. That's why we must destroy them."

"They give good Muslims a bad name."

"Yes they do." Sarya finished her coffee and put her mug down. "Thank you so much Vache, and I'll remember that coffee during the weeks to come!" she said with a big smile. "Now, I'll find Leila and we can talk while I rest."

Sarya fetched her rifle before going from house to house, until she spotted Leila, now wearing a blue blouse and black trousers, with a dark blue headscarf. Sarya went to the door and asked, "excuse me." Leila broke into a big smile and beckoned Sarya inside.

Sarya sat cross-legged opposite Leila. "How are you?" she asked.

"I'm feeling much better," Leila said. "Thank you for rescuing me."

"I came here to thank you for rescuing me," Sarya said. "When you grabbed my rifle."

Leila nodded. "We rescued each other." She looked at Sarya. "With a rifle you can protect yourself."

"Yes you can." Sarya thought about that, and to ask would do no harm. "I know you've been through a lot, but there's an opportunity for you to strike back. You can join the YPJ, like me."

"Can I?"

"Of course you can!" Sarya exclaimed. "Our armed forces aren't interested in race, gender or religion, and you speak our language so you can train alongside Kurdish women."

"And I can have a rifle and shoot DAESH like you?"

"There are many jobs in our army to support comrades on the front line, like the driver who saved us from that attack. All jobs in our army are important in the fight against DAESH."

"I understand."

"And if you join, you could be on the front line like me."

"I don't care if I have a rifle or not, as long as I'm helping to destroy those barbarians."

"There's more to an army than battles. The companionship of your colleagues is something I can't quite put words to. I think love, like the way you love your parents or your brother. It's wonderful to share food together, sing songs of victory together, and...."

"Feel love for each other."

"Yes."

"I need love in my life. I always feel sad, until I see you Sarya, and then I don't feel sad anymore. I think you're right that I should join the YPJ."

Sarya was pleased.

"How's your injury?" Leila asked.

"The doctor stitched my wound. He told me to rest for a few days before I return to battle."

"That's good. Tell me about yourself, Sarya."

"I'm age nineteen from the city of Amûdê. I have an older brother in university, and while I was in school I

168

followed this war and what DAESH were doing. My parents said I could volunteer for the YPJ when I finished school, which I passed in June. Then my friends and I volunteered, we were trained for a month, and now I'm here."

"Do you ever get scared?"

"Sometimes, especially before my first battle. When it actually happens you're too busy to be scared. The worst was when we were attacked on our way here."

"Have you killed many DAESH?"

As always Sarya felt her stomach churn; from thoughts of that terrorist who blew himself up, and the two terrorists bleeding to death on a concrete floor. Even the suicide truck driver, who was sure to die before Sarya killed him. Though they were DAESH; once they were loved by family and friends. "I don't like talking about that," she said quietly.

"You killed the man who abused me, and his friend."

"Yes I did. There are two others and that's all."

"Thank you for telling me that."

"It must be time for lunch," Sarya said. "Do you want to eat together?"

"Of course! And then I'll find out how to join the YPJ."

"I'm sure they have a recruitment office in Hasakah. After lunch, we can ask a driver to take you there."

Leila stood. "Let's have lunch together, and after lunch I'll join the YPJ."

They headed outside, and across Camp Martyr Diyako to the kitchen.

Chapter Fifteen

On a quiet day with only a sprained ankle from a football incident to treat, Vache was engrossed with his smartphone. In Paris the night before, there were a series of terrorist suicide attacks. Several incidents saw 130 dead and more than 400 injured. Unusually, DAESH took responsibility for that.

"That phone really has your attention today," Erna said as she took a seat.

Vache put it aside. "You heard what happened?"

"More attacks in France."

"Yes, but this is different. Up until now, Islamic extremist attacks have been by al-Qaeda, who did the Charlie Hebdo attack in Paris earlier this year. Last night's attacks are claimed by DAESH."

"What's the difference?" Erna asked.

"Al-Qaeda has always viewed their campaign as being for the soul of Islam. They pitted their version of Islam against the world, to provoke a response from Western countries. That forced Muslims to choose sides in what became a global war. DAESH believes that a defiled Islam must be purged of any deviance from the original teachings of Prophet Muhammad. They also believe that the final day of judgement by God is near, and that will follow the defeat of the army of Rome, which we assume to be Western Christians, by DAESH at Dabiq here in Syria."

Erna frowned. "What does that mean?"

"It means the reason for being for DAESH is to build a state in a specific place, Syria, and DAESH is more concerned with the souls of other Muslims than with the West. This is why their worst atrocities have been against Muslims in places like Raqqah, until last night."

"Could DAESH change direction and become like al-Qaeda? Could they force the West to respond in order for Muslims to choose sides?"

"This appears to be the case. The problem for the West is they now have two radical Islamic theocracies provoking them, which is quite literally double the trouble."

"DAESH have sensed they're losing this battle, and to win the souls of Muslims they need a different strategy."

Vache thought that was possible. "DAESH recruited by promising to be the winning side at a forthcoming day of judgement. For the naive, to be on the winning side at the end of times is a compelling reason to join, and to follow their ideology without deviation. That's not working so well now; or followers are abandoning DAESH as they lose more and more battles."

"As a Syrian, I'm all for DAESH moving their focus of operations away from here!" Erna exclaimed. "The West can look after themselves, sorry. No, not sorry, they started this.

If they never invaded Iraq; we never would have heard of DAESH."

"Not all the West; just the United States, Britain and Australia."

"I know. France opposed that war, and now they've been attacked. You're right Vache," Erna said. "For the West this is double the trouble."

It was indeed.

* * *

As soon as Adnan came home, he saw how sad Ranim looked, and he expected that. DAESH shut-down internet cafes that day.

"I'm sorry for both of us," Adnan said quietly.

She nodded her head in agreement. "We're cut-off from the world," she said. "I know how much you liked following the war of Kurds against DAESH, and particularly those Kurdish women soldiers."

"What we must do," Adnan said. "Is go out more and visit our friends. If we can't do that online then we must do that in person."

"Yes, we will do that," she said.

"But I'll miss following the war and seeing DAESH get defeated."

"You're more interested in those women in uniform!" Ranim laughed.

For some reason Adnan found that stirring, which was odd. He loved femininity, while women soldiers in uniform with rifles were the polar opposite of femininity. "Could you join an army, if you had the opportunity?" he asked.

"I would like to say yes I could, but no I couldn't. I just couldn't shoot a man"

"Why do you think they can?"

"We had some Kurds here in Raqqah until they fled when DAESH took over, but I didn't know them well. We know in Rojava they've encouraged women to join their army, and numbers may give women strength through comradeship. What I can't imagine doing on my own; maybe I could do if lots of women are doing it too. Also I think Kurds have been victimised for a long time, by Assad and by others before him, and they have a culture of fighting for survival. This would explain why they can defeat DAESH when Arab armies can't."

"They're natural warriors," Adnan said.

"Both men and women."

"They will liberate us from oppression."

"This is why DAESH shut down those cafes. They couldn't afford Raqqah seeing them get defeated; village by village and town by town. This is a Kurdish victory, and a victory for all of us."

Yet again Adnan was stunned. His smart wife had seen right through DAESH's motives and exposed the core of their fragility. And in doing so she'd given them hope in the midst of despair. For sure, she was smarter than he. For sure, many of those Kurdish women soldiers were more than smart enough to win the war against DAESH. For sure, the defeat of DAESH would come in time.

* * *

Sarya climbed out of the Toyota, grabbed her rifle from the back seat; slung it over her shoulder and thanked the driver. She wandered amongst comrades, until she spotted Mina and the rest. She went to them.

"Silav Mina," she greeted.

"Silav Sarya," Mina greeted in reply. "How are you?"

"I'm good now. You would have heard what happened."

"Agir and you saw that suicide car. He ran to warn others while you were injured when it blew-up. Sadly, Agir was killed."

Sarya immediately felt sick. Terribly, terribly sick. "I'm sorry to hear that," she said quietly.

"War can be tough at times."

"Agir is a martyr to our cause," Sarya said. At his home town of Ras al-Ayn he would receive a grand funeral for a martyr, like so many before him.

"Agir is a martyr to our cause," Mina repeated. "You're now part of Team Martyr Agir."

Sarya felt that was appropriate.

"Sarya," Mina said. "This is Havel Soran, who's been a driver for the past two years. He's now part of Team Martyr Agir."

"Rojbash Havel Soran," Sarya greeted.

"Rojbash Havel Sarya," he said, before kissing her cheeks.

Soran was older, well into his thirties, and he wore a wedding ring. As a driver he knew what he was getting himself in for, which was good.

"You have a scar," Olan said with a big smile.

Sarya smiled. "Yes, I'm scarred from battle, but it's only a small scar. I was lucky."

"Sometimes we make our own luck," Mina said.

"Sometimes," Sarya repeated, while contemplating the meaning of that. Was Agir reckless, maybe?

"Did you discover anything useful over the past few days?"

Sarya thought. "They have decent food and I even had a mug of coffee!"

Keya playfully punched her shoulder. "While we had tinned chicken and bottled water!"

"Yes you did. Other than the food, I'm glad to be back with my comrades. What's happening here?"

"We're still taking villages, and obviously the main objective is al-Shaddadah," Mina said. "There we'll encounter proper DAESH resistance. I don't know when that is, and I'll

tell you when I find out. Tomorrow, we take the village of –
I've forgotten the name. Ah yes, Qana. Tomorrow, we take
Qana."

"There's one thing," Sarya remembered. "DAESH
tried to use a suicide truck on the camp."

Mina nodded her head. "That's interesting. They're
feeling desperate and they're resorting to desperate tactics."

"There's no doubt we have the upper hand, with
support in the air by the Coalition."

"DAESH don't have an air force, but they do have
fanatics. We'll have to be alert for more suicide attacks.
Enough of that!" Mina hugged Sarya by her shoulders.
"Sarya's back and our team's complete."

Sarya felt loved, and that was one thing she'd missed.
She hoped, no, she knew her friend Leila would find love
through the path she'd chosen. With love, nothing else
matters.

Chapter Sixteen

Day by day and week by week, the Syrian Democratic Force pushed ever closer to al-Shaddadah, gradually encircling the town from the east and from the west. There they paused while support bases were established closer to the front line, and more tabûr were brought into Operation Wrath of Khabur.

On February 16, 2016; the operation started on a winter's cold dawn, overrunning multiple villages and giving DAESH no chance. Whenever stiff resistance was encountered, airstrikes were called in. Over the next two days they closed on the town; taking more villages and pushing to within a few kilometres of the outskirts of al-Shaddadah. The following day, the 19th, some from the SDF entered al-Shaddadah, very much damaged from airstrikes on DAESH positions in the town. It was a town about two-thirds the size of Amûdê, where ordinary people had suffered badly. Airstrikes inevitably resulted in civilian casualties, while a makeshift cross on a power pylon outside the ruins of the courthouse showed that rule by DAESH was particularly barbaric.

Despite destruction all around; locals celebrated liberation. Women discarded their black abayas and niqabs, which littered streets and roads. Team Martyr Agir was split up for a while, with Sarya and other SDF women helping

Yazidi women from what they called a slave market. The Yazidi women's relief after a year and a half of sex slavery was almost overwhelming, but some were so young that Sarya had difficulty dealing with her task. She wanted to be happy and positive for those poor women, but she felt suffocated by the darkness around her. Some, after a year and a half of being bought and sold by their DAESH masters, were still only 13 or 14 years old. Sarya could help them to busses to take them to refugee camps, but always she wondered what future those girls could ever have in life. They were orphans, probably with no living relatives, now sent to camps where at least they would get food and shelter. But always Sarya wondered what their futures could be. Almost certainly, refugee camps for many, many years. Some of the older girls, 17 or 18 like Leila, had a better future. When some of those young women were rescued by what they called women soldiers, like Leila they wanted to be soldiers themselves. They wanted to turn the tables on those who'd abused them. But saddest was the fate of women older still. Women in their twenties and thirties were widowed; their husbands surely massacred, and who knew what happened to their children? In the primes of their lives they'd lost everything. They were rescued but they faced a bleak future.

After the last of the hundreds of women departed, Sarya walked through the bombed remains of the slave market. Abayas discarded, and strangely many items of fancy

179

underwear, including colourful, padded bras and even see-through negligees. DAESH dressed their young slaves like whores, and then covered them from head to toe when they went outside, only to strip them in privacy; no doubt to salivate over their whore-like clothes. Sarya caught up with the rest of her team defusing IEDs, which littered much of the town. There she sat and watched them at work.

"How was it?" Mina asked.

Sarya didn't have to pretend fake bravado. "They tore my heart," she said.

Mina sat beside her. "We rescued them."

"To what future?"

"No longer will they be abused."

Sarya looked at her commander, and that was true. "Their futures will be better than their pasts."

"They must be."

Sarya surveyed the ruined town, now with SDF flags flying. "How did we defeat DAESH in three days?" she asked in wonder. "Americans said this would take six weeks."

"There are still pockets of DAESH resistance."

"But only pockets of resistance. Mostly we've got the villages in this region, and now this city."

"I know what you mean and I don't know. Clearly airstrikes played a part, but airstrikes don't win battles or wars."

"DAESH defeated the Iraqi army supported by their airforce, and then DAESH defeated Assad's army supported by his airforce, and DAESH defeated other opposition armies here in Syria."

"DAESH were the best of a bad lot, until they met Kurds supported by Coalition airforces."

"Do you know what happens next?" Sarya asked.

"Next is Raqqah, similar to here. Villages in that region, closing on that city. Raqqah is the capital of their caliphate, and they'll defend that to their last fanatic. It's a city of two-hundred and twenty thousand, and that will be a battle like you or I have never fought before."

"Perhaps DAESH withdrew men from here, to defend their capital of Raqqah?"

Mina smiled brightly. "Young Sarya; you have a soldiers mind."

Sarya smiled at that compliment. She liked Mina, a lot.

"Sarya," Mina said. "Once we finish clearing these IEDs, I want the team to take leave in turns."

Sarya didn't want to leave the battlefield, but she understood. Raqqah was coming, and she needed to be recovered and refreshed for that. "I can wash my uniform and have a bath, and to be sure I need both!"

Mina laughed. "We all need a break, wash our clothes, and definitely a bath."

* * *

Vache watched the film, and it was both fascinating and awfully depressing.

"What's that you've got," Erna said.

"Sit beside me and watch, because this is interesting,"

Vache moved the slider to the start of the clip, and played it from there. Deliberately distorted voices gave the clip an air of unreality, but the sight of hair dye boxes with model's faces scribbled over in black was even more unreal. Women in the street, all in black with a little slit for vision, looked ghastly as they drifted along. Vache knew women liked to show their faces, as the woman filming said, which made being covered in shapeless black garments even harder for many women to bear. It was odd to see a cage at Naeem Roundabout, and terrible to think that cage was for the stoning of women. Women killed in such a brutal manner committed adultery, which might be as simple as pre-marital sex or even just dating. Pre-marital sex was once common enough across all cultures in Syria; especially between those who planned to marry one day.

The film then went to the district where they once lived, and now those expensive houses and apartments were occupied by foreign DAESH terrorists, who were almost solely responsible for the oppression and brutality that was a daily part of life in Raqqah, and in other parts of Syria. It was hard to imagine how the men at the top of DAESH could be so twisted and cruel as to inflict such a barbaric life on so many innocent people.

Towards the end the woman took off part of her layers of garments, with the camera filming from behind so her face remained hidden. What wasn't hidden was her thick, shock of beautiful black hair as she rearranged it. What a shame to hide such beautiful hair.

"Well, that was something," Erna said. "The wet weather with mud and slush had Raqqah looking at its worst, but beyond that their treatment of women is terrible. Raqqah wasn't cosmopolitan like bigger cities, but it was a free and pleasant, multi-cultural city. Older Arab women tended to dress conservatively and mostly wore hijabs to hide their hair. Younger Arab women tended to dress Western, and sometimes they wore hijabs and sometimes not. You always knew Kurds from their darker complexions, and older Kurdish women mostly dressed conservatively while young Kurdish women mostly dressed more Western, but Kurds didn't bother with hijabs, although some wore a scarf which still showed their typically long, black hair. We Christians, Assyrians mostly and a few Armenians, dressed as we chose, and we didn't look out of place because of the casually dressed young Arab and young Kurdish women around us. Arab women can sometimes be very attractive and Kurdish women too, and it was nice to see that on the streets of Raqqah."

Vache was surprised. "You admire women?" he asked.

"Of course I do! I don't know if there's God, but if there is then His most attractive creation was woman. You admire women I'm sure, and there's no harm in that."

"Of course I admire women, and there's no harm in that. I might admire a sports car parked in the street, but that doesn't mean I'm going to steal it."

"What we saw is more than hiding women from men's temptation. Women bring life into the world, and women can choose whichever man to do that with. Beyond that, women can do almost all things that men can do. Women can have it all, which is why men invented the patriarchy to control women, and especially to control women's reproduction."

"It's ironic that Kurdish women, who are Sunni Muslim, are dismantling the patriarchy."

"With the help of Kurdish men in the higher echelons of the PYD here, and the PKK[5] in Turkey."

"A liberated woman makes a more complete life's partner to men, and we benefit from that."

"Do you?" Erna asked.

"Oh yes," Vache said. "Discussions like this, or working together like we do."

"A more active and confident sexual partner?"

---

[5] PKK – Partiya Karkerén Kurdistané or Kurdistan Worker's Party

"Absolutely." Vache thought about that. "Controlling women like DAESH means you don't have to satisfy women sexually," he said. "Under DAESH, women can't meet men except through arranged marriages, and once married they're men's possession, so it doesn't matter if sex is good or bad for those wives."

"You think this sort of treatment is a sign of sexual insecurity?"

"I think this sort of treatment is a sign of men's insecurity at many levels, including sexual."

"I'm sorry that the men and women of Raqqah are forced to live like that," Erna said.

"Me too."

"We're doing the right thing by helping to bring this to an end."

That bleak film was proof they were doing the right thing.

Chapter Seventeen

The regular executions after Friday's prayer brought a new low for their DAESH tormenters. There, in al-Dallah Roundabout, were three men and a boy, quite literally a boy, aged about seven. The first man had committed sodomy, with who they did not say and it could have even been his wife. He was shot in the head. The next man had committed apostasy, which meant holding an alternative religious view, and he was shot in the head. The young boy was guilty of insulting divinity, which Adnan assumed to be swearing, and he was shot in the head. The last man was guilty of thieving, and with much screaming and shouting, his left hand was cut off, and he was forced to hold that hand in his right hand. Then he was taken away, hopefully for medical treatment.

With that tragedy over, Adnan walked with Abdul, back to the sheep market. They walked in silence because conversations overheard could get them into trouble; even execution for apostasy, which was a catch-all for less than total belief in DAESH's sick version of Islam.

They got to the sheep market, where Adnan was more troubled than usual for a Friday afternoon, despite pleasant spring weather. Friday the 6th of May, 2016; and soon the endless heat of summer would be upon them.

"I don't know about that boy," Adnan said, for something to say.

"Who hasn't sworn?" Abdul asked.

"But a boy that age?"

"I know," Abdul sighed. "It was during a football game."

"So he missed a goal in a friendly game in his street, swore, and was shot in the head?"

"Like we've all done at some time or other."

"What about his parents? How much have they suffered?" Adnan asked.

Adnan then was quiet. He wanted to say 'this will be over soon', but that was a step too far. Part of Adnan wanted to reassure his employer, who was a good and decent man, but another part of him knew those words could get him executed if the wrong person ever heard. So he held his words back, because those special words could only be shared with Ranim. That evening, when he told her what he saw. A seven year old boy shot in the head for exclaiming 'God' during a football game.

* * *

Sarya climbed out and thanked her comrade driver, before slinging her rifle over her shoulder. She hesitated for a moment before knocking on the door. That door opened slowly; then Mama grabbed Sarya hard, and kissed her hard too.

"You're home," Mama said.

"Yes I'm home," Sarya replied, while Mama's embrace nearly knocked her off her feet.

"Come inside."

Sarya entered a room that hadn't changed, but it felt like years since she'd been there. Papa grabbed her shoulders and looked her in her eyes.

"How are you?" he asked.

"I'm fine," Sarya said. "I'll get rid of this and get changed."

She went to her room which hadn't changed, but also felt like years. There she leaned her rifle in the corner; stripped off her flak jacket, her dirty uniform and headscarf, and left them on her bed to be dealt with later. She pulled on a blouse and trousers from her chest, before returning to the living room and waiting awkwardly.

"How are you?" Mama said.

"I'm fine," Sarya repeated.

"You have a scar," Papa said.

"Pardon? Oh, that. Yes I do."

"I was about to serve dinner," Mama said.

"I can help," Sarya offered.

"Nonsense!" Mama exclaimed.

Sarya sat on the floor and Papa sat opposite. Silence.

"You can tell me as much or as little as you want," he said.

Sarya thought about what to say during the drive home. "You've read books and memoirs about war," she said. "I can't add to what you already know, except war has a lot of time waiting for something to happen, and short bursts of activity where hours seem like minutes. Then you're waiting with your comrades again. The one difference in our war is being a man or a woman doesn't matter. The men can be nearly twice your age and from a different generation; yet they put their lives in your hands and know that you'll do the right thing for them and for the team." She looked deeply at Papa. "Our new way in Rojava works in this war."

"That's good to hear. I've followed our progress."

"I knew you would. We will defeat DAESH," Sarya said. "They may fight to their last terrorist, but we will win."

"This will take time."

"This will take time with many casualties, but we will win."

Mama brought out plates of biryani, dolma, bread, and then glasses of tea. Sarya sipped her tea before she had some of Mama's wonderful cooking.

"This is what I miss the most," Sarya said. "At base we all take turns cooking, even the men, while away from base the food is quite horrible."

"I would like to see men cooking," Mama said.

Sarya smiled at that thought. "They learn," she said.

"You have a scar."

"I was hit by something from an explosion and a doctor put stitches for me. It's nothing."

"How long are you home?"

"For a week. After we eat I'll bathe, and I must wash my uniform too. Tomorrow, because we have to spend time together.

"And visit your uncles, aunts and cousins."

"Yes, I must do that." Sarya pictured men returning home from war as it has always been; re-connecting with family and friends while on leave. Now a teenage girl can return home from war, and be evasive about suicide cars or shooting DAESH terrorists at close range. War has always been hard for soldiers, but this war was different. She remembered Leila Khider and her terrible suffering. Every single member of her family was killed and she was raped many times. And the hundreds of women from al-Shaddadah; who'd all suffered similar, terrible fates.

Sarya looked at Papa. "War is bad," she said. "But in this war, there's never been a stronger case of right and wrong. I know that more strongly now than when I volunteered."

"The great Kurdish warrior Saladin always warned against shedding blood, indulging in it, or making a habit of it, for blood never sleeps."

Sarya agreed with that. Having conquered large parts of Syria, DAESH behaved barbarically and united many

190

powerful enemies against them. That was their downfall. Sarya didn't know what to say. Could she comment on someone as great as Saladin? "I understand," she said quietly.

"I'm sure you do," Papa said.

Sarya nodded while she ate some dolma and sipped her tea. In the corner of the room the television, which once formed the centre of her family's evenings, sat eternally silent. For many years it had been nothing more than a propaganda tool for the Assad regime.

Sarya finished eating, thanked Mama for such a wonderful meal, because Mama was a great cook. Then she bathed after almost a year of just washing, and sometimes not having the opportunity to wash often enough. She lay in the bath where it was very, very quiet. Always around her were the men and women of the SDF, and especially her comrades in Team Martyr Agir. After a while Sarya climbed from cooling water, dressed in fresh underwear and the clothes she'd chosen before, and told her parents she was going out.

Amûdê on a mild, spring evening had not changed one bit. Sarya knew her people's history better than most, or probably more than what they would care to admit. In what is now Turkey, some Kurds participated in the terrible genocide against Armenians. But unlike Turks, Kurds, especially the PKK, officially recognised that genocide and condemned those Kurds who'd participated in it. Armenians responded positively to that, and a great weight was lifted from both people.

In more recent times in the 1930s, Kurds attacked Armenians and Assyrians to the north of Syria. In response, French Christians attacked Muslim Kurds, and in revenge, Kurds from Turkey attacked Christian Assyrians in what was Amuda, and drove them away. Now the city was Kurdish Amûdê, the result of three large cultures: Turk, Kurd and Armenian, all laying claim over one area of land. On the Syrian side of the Turkish border, Kurd had rated secondary to Arab for almost a century. Until this war, Sarya's language and even her name were illegal. On the other side of the border, Kurds continued to be persecuted by Turks. In Iraq, Kurds had a degree of autonomy in an Arab-majority country. Overall, Sarya's people were the largest nation in the world without a state.

Only then did Sarya recognise something. One hundred years ago, Turks killed Armenian men before marching Armenian women and children to camps, with many dying on the way. Most surviving desirable Armenian women were then sold as sex slaves. A year and a half ago, DAESH went to the lands of the Yazidi where they killed all men and old women, before taking younger women to be used as sex slaves. That was almost the same as the Armenian genocide. Clearly DAESH wanted to destroy Yazidi, just like Turks once wanted to destroy Armenians.

Sarya turned a corner to see a group of boys noisily played football on a side-street, which was like men at a camp when nothing else was happening. They had to be active and competing against one-another. Sarya watched them, and her lesson in jineology suddenly made sense. Men tended to be competitive where women tended to be cooperative, and society was fashioned by men to be competitive rather than cooperative, within which women could never be equal. The SDF was cooperative rather than competitive, so talented women like Mina could rise to the rank of commander. She watched those boys for a while, before turning another corner and heading towards home. There she would sleep on a clean, soft bed, dressed in pyjamas no less, and not sleep in her uniform on dirt or concrete. Mina was right; she needed that.

* * *

Leaflets fluttered through the streets of Raqqah, dropped by white drones circling overhead. Adnan grabbed one as it fell close by, and it told him that air attacks were coming soon, and they should leave Raqqah. It was the 20th of May, 2016; and Adnan wondered what soon meant, and how long it would take for Kurdish forces to liberate Raqqah. Many more DAESH militants patrolled than normal, and that was no coincidence. Adnan thrust the leaflet into his pocket and walked home.

He showed his leaflet to Ranim, but she had one from when she went out that day with Nour.

"What do you think we should do?" Adnan asked.

She sat and he sat beside her. "I don't know," she said. "Clearly it's dangerous to stay but DAESH won't let me leave, and now it seems nobody is allowed to leave. DAESH are patrolling streets in great numbers, and I expect they guard roads out of the city too, and they will shoot us if we try to leave."

"What's Nour going to do?"

"She's going to talk with her husband."

Adnan had an idea. "Let's see what other people do. If they get away then we can leave, but if they have problems then we will stay."

"Yes, we'll do that," Ranim said. She playfully ruffled his hair, and that said that was a good idea.

The next morning Adnan headed to the sheep market for work, but he saw DAESH were digging fields beside the road; probably for mines. If roads were guarded and fields were mined, then nobody could leave.

"What do you want?" a voice asked.

Adnan turned to face a DAESH militant. "I work past there," Adnan said.

"You don't work past there anymore."

Adnan nodded and returned home. While he walked he realised he had a problem. He was out of a job in a city where there was no work to be had. He reached home and let himself in.

"DAESH wouldn't let you go to work at the outskirts," Ranim said rather than asked.

"Yes, that's right," Adnan said.

"I'm not surprised, and they won't let Abdul bring his truck in either."

Adnan sat on the couch. There was one possibility. "I'll ring Papa," he said. Adnan rang and Papa answered a few moments later. Adnan explained his problem, and Papa understood. He said to come to work at the cafe, now. There's not much work, but there's enough. He thanked Papa and hung up.

"Paying my wages will make life tougher for Papa and Mama," Adnan said. "But Papa didn't hesitate."

"We're all family," Ranim said.

"That's right. I'll go now."

Adnan reached the cafe about ten minutes later.

"Thanks Papa," he said.

"Enough with the thanks!" Papa said. "You did the right thing at the time, but now things have changed. As long as we both earn enough for rent and food, then we'll get by."

"That's right," Adnan said. "How's business?"

"Mostly DAESH, and there are more DAESH than before."

"That's good then."

"As long as you don't mind serving those...."

"What choice do we have?" Adnan looked around and nobody else was around. "I'm sure the Kurds will beat DAESH, and then life will be back to normal."

"I think Kurds have driven DAESH from other towns and cities, and they've come here for a final stand."

"That's possible Papa. Ranim and I are going to see what other people do. If they get away then we'll leave, but if they have trouble then we'll stay."

"That's a good idea, Adnan. That's a very good idea."

Four customers came into the cafe, all DAESH, and Adnan went to serve them. Papa was right. The hardest thing was serving these sub-humans with accents not from Syria. They'd come to his country; they'd come to his city, and they'd destroyed it. Now Kurds and their Western allies were going to bring war to Raqqah.

That war came the next day; on Friday the 20th of May. Aircraft after aircraft roared overhead, and missiles exploded on targets all over and beyond the city. At times the targets were so close the ground shook, and still the attacks continued. This was worse, much worse than the Jordanian airstrikes in retribution for the murder of their pilot. Buildings in many parts of the city were bombed to destruction, and there must have been causalities. It would not be possible to bomb so many buildings, presumably DAESH targets, and not injure and kill civilians living nearby.

For sure, the Kurdish army and their Western allies had brought war to Raqqah. By late afternoon airstrikes eased, and Adnan felt safe enough to leave the cafe and head home. He was convinced they had to leave, because surely to stay was a death sentence. But that was a decision they both had to make, in a marriage of equals.

Adnan stared out the living room window. "Do you think we should go?" he asked.

"It's true it's dangerous at the moment," Ranim said from behind. "But we still don't know what DAESH will do, and we don't know how many more attacks there will be. Nothing happened to either of us and there were no missile attacks in this neighbourhood, so I think we should stay until we know more."

That sounded reasonable. Adnan turned around. "Alright," he said.

"Now, I've cooked klbbeh bll sanleh with fattoush, if you're hungry."

Adnan wasn't particularly hungry when he got home, but that changed his mind. Minced meat with pine nuts and kibbeh, with a salad of tomato, cucumber and radish. That was enough to charge any man's appetite! While he ate that delicious meal, he wondered what to do that evening. It was pleasant spring weather, but an evening walk along the streets hadn't been possible for a long time. There was always one thing, and sometimes Adnan wondered if DAESH realised what they'd done. With no television, no cinema, no music, no internet and not being allowed out in the evenings, there wasn't much left, not that Adnan was complaining. Well there was one other thing, and then making love before they slept.

"Something's got your fancy," Ranim said.

"Can you guess?" Adnan asked.

"You want to go a nightclub? No? A walk in the park? No? I wonder what it could be?"

Adnan went to the bedroom to fetch his pack of cards. He sat at the table before looking across at Ranim who looked disappointed. "There's always time for a game of cards," he said, and laughed.

"And after the game?"

That wasn't subtle. "What do you really want, my love?" he asked.

"I want to do something in honour of our DAESH masters, who would be apoplectic with rage if they found out."

"What?" Adnan asked; really curious about that.

Ranim walked around the table and whispered in his ear. Adnan was shocked.

"Do you really want to?" he asked.

"We've not done that before," Ranim said.

"How?'

"There's oil left over from the salad, and we go from there."

Adnan contemplated that. "You're right," he said. "They would be apoplectic with rage."

"Does that excite you?"

"Absolutely."

Adnan thought it will be difficult to keep a straight face tomorrow, in front of those ever so serious foreign zealots. So yes, for sure! He left his cards on the table and followed Ranim to their bedroom.

* * *

Adnan dreamt of gunfire, like a movie on television. That was odd because he hadn't seen a movie or watched television for so long. Perhaps his thoughts had drifted to those simple pleasures of past times. He sat up in bed. That wasn't a movie.

"What is it?" Ranim asked.

"I heard gunfire," Adnan said. He checked his smartphone: five-thirteen. Early dawn. He wondered. "Would someone try to leave the city at this time of morning?"

"When DAESH might be asleep, but aren't."

Adnan went to the living room and peered outside, but saw nothing in the faint light of a morning just arriving.

"If something's happened my love," Ranim said from behind. "We should keep away. We'll find out soon enough."

Adnan returned to bed, but knew he wouldn't sleep. Eventually it was time to get up, shower, dress, and have breakfast of bread with yoghurt, and tea.

"You should go out with Nour," he said. "While you can."

"I will," Ranim said.

He kissed her, and went down the stairs. There he stopped in shock. The Khalil family from upstairs; all four of them. Lying on the street; shot to death. Adnan never realised there would be so much blood. He looked around nervously but saw no DAESH militants, yet there must have been a sniper hiding somewhere. Adnan shoved his hands into his pockets and headed away; deep in thought. Already it was too late. And if they could get away from the neighbourhood, there were only five roads out of Raqqah: two to the north, one to the west, one to the east and one to the south, across the river. Adnan was sure those roads would be guarded, and bridges too, and fields around the city were already mined. They were trapped. They couldn't have left earlier because women weren't allowed out of the city, now they were even more trapped. Adnan decided to tell Papa, be strong for Ranim, and hope they would get by. Overhead, Adnan heard that sound like thunder which wasn't thunder. That was more aircraft approaching, for more missile attacks. Adnan walked faster to the cafe which at least gave the illusion of safety, even if that building would collapse and kill them if it was bombed. In that cafe Adnan would serve DAESH, who were nonplussed by the destruction of Raqqah; their self-proclaimed capital. DAESH who seemed nonplussed that eventually they would lose. DAESH who seemed determined to take many Raqqah civilians with them, when surely they were near their end.

At the cafe, Adnan told Papa about the family who were shot trying to leave in the early morning. Then two DAESH militants came in and ordered coffee each. Adnan made their drinks at the counter while they talked at a nearby table, and that conversation was interesting. They mentioned 800 dollars per person, and that could mean only one thing: the going rate for a bribe to get out of Raqqah. He served their coffees and received a tip of five dollars, for all the good that would do. Nobody in his or Ranim's families had anything like 800 dollars each, having survived on reduced incomes while the economy of Raqqah steadily declined over the past few years. Those DAESH militants left and Adnan went to the kitchen.

"I overheard some DAESH talking," Adnan told Papa. "To get out of Raqqah, they want eight-hundred US dollars per person."

Papa's face changed, and it looked like he stifled a swear word. "We don't have that much money," he eventually said.

"Doctors and lawyers have that much, but not us."

"Doctors left long ago, and lawyers too, but there may be some who have that much. My son," Papa said, as a missile exploded somewhere in the distance. "We're stuck here for better or for worse. And I'm sure we'll see worse before we see anything better."

Another missile struck and another building was destroyed, and surely they would see worse before they saw anything better.

Chapter Eighteen

Sarya stood behind the sandbag wall, and used her binoculars to scan the plain for any signs of activity. To keep her mind active and not lose concentration, she paced from one end of the wall to the other, while staring across the plain. Behind her, the village of Aalou bustled as inhabitants put order into the chaos that inevitably followed a battle. Despite damage to some homes and shops, the people of Aalou were much relieved to be liberated from DAESH, and their liberators being Kurds didn't matter at all. Although a small village, many had been beaten for not following DAESH's rules on clothing, beards and prayer. Sarya was surprised to discover the abaya and niqab were Saudi Arabian garments, and Syrian women didn't wear such clothes until the DAESH invasion. In Syria, merely covering their hair was sufficient, and not all did that.

Not only were the inhabitants of Aalou pleased to be liberated, they were even more pleased the SDF stayed to protect them. Aalou was the current front line as DAESH were squeezed closer and closer to their capital of Raqqah. There was always a chance DAESH would attempt to retake some of the ground they were losing, which was why Sarya scanned the plains for sign of movement.

There Sarya spotted a plume of dust. She focussed her binoculars to see a white van speeding across the plain and closing on the village. That van wasn't DAESH. Well, probably not DAESH.

"What is it?" Mina asked from behind.

"Supplies," Sarya said, while she kept them in sight. There was a slight chance they were DAESH masking as SDF. In the background, Mina used her scrambled radio to confirm they were supplies, and Sarya relaxed.

The Toyota pulled up beyond the sandbag wall, and happy comrades jumped out to unlock the rear of the van. Sarya resumed her scanning of the plain.

"Sarya!" a woman's voice called.

Sarya turned around to face Leila, looking fine in her uniform. "Leila!" Sarya exclaimed. "It's great to see you."

"It's great to see you too. You were right about the YPJ, and you were right about not needing to be on the front line."

"You're on the front line now."

"That's true, and our supplies will help you to defeat DAESH."

"That's right."

Sarya turned back to the scan the plain as Leila came alongside. "You can help me," Sarya said. "This is the front line and DAESH could advance on us anytime."

"So you watch."

"We watch in turns, and this is my turn."

"What's that?" Leila asked, while pointing across the plain.

Sarya used her binoculars on something dark, and brought that into focus. She saw a truck in dark colours, escorted by several utilities. DAESH!

"Come with me," Sarya said, and ran to centre of the village to find Mina. "Stay here," Sarya told Leila, before grabbing Mina. "DAESH are approaching; I think with a Technical with artillery, and several utilities."

"Most likely more Technicals, and utilities carrying terrorists," Mina said, while she ran with Sarya to the sandbag wall. Mina used her binoculars to scan the scene, before running back to the village. In no time, all were against that wall, and as always, their Kalashnikovs and their PK machine gun didn't have the range.

"Use the RPG, Sarya," Mina said, while she sniped with her AK47.

Sarya leaned her rifle against the wall, and went to the centre of the village once more. Their supplies were in the ruins of the one destroyed house, including an anti-tank missile launcher. An RPG-7 wouldn't disable a modern tank, but it was good enough against a truck with an artillery gun on its tray. Nearby was Leila.

"Leila," Sarya said. "Grab a few RPG missiles and come with me."

Sarya, RPG in hand, returned to the sandbag wall where she saw the artillery Technical do a big turn to face the gun towards Aalou village. About 20 DAESH terrorists jumped from utilities; ready to advance under artillery fire while being protected by large-calibre, utility-mounted machine guns. Sarya fed a missile into the front of the RPG, stood behind the wall, aimed, and squeezed the trigger. Boom, whoosh, but just a spray of earth about 10 metres off-target. She put the RPG down to load it, and saw Leila watching.

"Bring more missiles," Sarya said, just as the DAESH artillery shelled towards the village, with a shell exploding somewhere beyond. Sarya stood and aimed, but again she missed. What was wrong with her? Still DAESH artillery shelled, with exploding shells much closer. For a third time Sarya stood, aimed, and as steadily as she could, she squeezed the trigger.

The explosion was quite massive, and the truck quite devastated. The gun on the tray was lopsided and pointing at the sky. Now DEASH advanced on foot, to come under rifle and machine gun fire from Sarya's comrades. DAESH returned fire, with their chants of 'Allahu akbar' as they shot clear and distinct.

Some DAESH terrorists advanced towards the right where the village was less protected.

"Barî and Keya come with me," Mina ordered, as she spread her meagre troops across a line too thin to defend. The three ran; heads down, while Sarya loaded another missile into the RPG. The battle was totally intense, with machine guns on the DAESH Technicals firing near continuously to protect their advancing troops, who also stopped and shot as they closed. Sarya glanced across and watched Mina cross from the sandbag wall to the earth bank, and suddenly crumple to the ground holding her leg. She'd been shot through that narrow gap! Heart beating fast, Sarya stood once more, aimed the RPG at the closer of the two Technicals; with bullets now whizzing past her head and thudding into sandbags at her chest, and fired. The Technical literally leapt into the air, and was reduced to a ruin. Once more Sarya loaded a missile, stood, aimed at the other Technical again under machine gun fire, shot and missed. Again she aimed, shot and missed, and on the third attempt she hit the ground just in front of the gun to spray it with earth. That must have been good enough to disable the gun, because they stopped firing. Sarya put the RPG down and ran to Mina who'd been pulled aside by the men of their team now firing on approaching DAESH terrorists.

Sarya knelt with Mina's bloody leg visible through her torn uniform. Remembering her training, Sarya tore at the uniform to fully expose Mina's wound, and then grabbed Mina's bandage from her flak jacket. She wrapped that bandage tight, and strapped it even tighter with Mina's tourniquet.

"You'll be fine," Sarya said, before she went to her rifle and poked it through a sniping hole in the wall. There she picked out DAESH terrorists. One fell from her rifle fire and a DAESH colleague dragged him out of range. Further along, Olan sprayed DAESH using the PK with the belt guided by Soran, and from her vantage point Sarya saw their advance falter with ever more causalities. For once DAESH were in the open and attacking a well-defended position, but they didn't have the tactics to carry that out. In fact they were a total shambles as one almost shot his colleagues with a rocket! Soon DAESH retreated to their utilities dragging injured colleagues with them; leaving behind a damaged Technical artillery truck, two damaged machine gun Technicals, and a few bodies. Sarya kept sniping to further reduce their moral, as did her comrades. One machine gun Technical was still relatively intact and probably drivable, so Sarya exchanged her rifle for the RPG once more. When not under fire; aiming and shooting was easy, and she blew it up. That was the end of it, and DAESH drove away in their surviving utilities.

Sarya sat with her back to the sandbag wall, and her mind blank. Only then did she realise Leila was still there. "You saved me again," Sarya said.

"You saved me too," Leila said, before hugging Sarya. Sarya loved Leila like a sister, if she had a sister.

There was one thing more important than all others. "We must get our commander to the field hospital without delay," Sarya said.

"We can do that," Leila said.

Sarya went to Mina.

"Olan and Soran," Sarya said. "Carry Mina to the supply van, and they'll take her to the field hospital."

"Wait a moment," Mina said. She reached to her shoulder and gave her radio to Sarya. "You know how to use this.'

"I do."

Sarya watched Olan and Soran take Mina to the back of the van. There Leila slammed the rear doors before they drove away. Sarya followed their dust trail for a time, before sitting once more.

"That was intense," Olan said flatly.

"Mina will recover, I'm sure," Sarya said. But only if Mina didn't lose too much blood before she got treated. It was a long way to camp. Sarya hoped her commander and friend would survive.

Chapter Nineteen

Olan came into the village, where Sarya drank from a bottle of tepid water in the shade of the ruined house.

"Sarya," he said. "There's a vehicle approaching."

Sarya put her bottle down to jog to the sandbag wall. There Keya had his binoculars trained on an approaching dust cloud. "Single vehicle?" she asked.

"Yes," Keya said.

Sarya took the radio and pressed the transmit button. "Havel Sarya Goran from Team Martyr Agir to vehicle approaching the village of Aalou. Please identify yourself."

"Havel Irem with a visitor for Team Martyr Agir," a woman's voice replied.

"Thank you Havel Irem."

That was odd. Sarya went to where an inevitable Toyota Landcruiser rattled into the village. The passenger door opened, and a YPJ comrade emerged. She looked familiar but Sarya couldn't quite place her, and then she did. Komutan Rojda Felat! Sarya felt weak at the knees. The team, except for Keya on duty, gathered around, and for some reason, the sight of Rojda Felat drew everyone to her. That reason was charisma.

"I've come here today with good news," Komutan Rojda said. "Komutan Mina is well and she'll recover from her injuries, although her rehabilitation will take a long time.

Mina's recovery will take a year or even longer, but she will recover. I've also come to congratulate you on your victory yesterday, where you defeated a force far greater in size than your own. You should all feel proud about what you achieved. Now Havel Sarya; I'd like a word with you."

Sarya stepped forward, only to have Komutan Rojda wander through the village and away from the rest of the team. "The doctor told me that had you not given the first aid you did; Mina would have died," she said. "You acted well and are a credit to the YPJ. Mina wants you to consider being her permanent replacement, and before you say anything, I'll tell you what she said. She said that your bravery goes without saying, but more than bravery, you think through the most appropriate responses before acting, which makes you a very effective soldier and will make you an effective leader. She also said that you have the absolute respect of every member of this team. So what do you say, Havel Sarya?"

"I will stand to be elected as commander of this team," Sarya said automatically, while feeling she wasn't worthy for such a role. Two men were older and more experienced than she, and surely they were more worthy.

"I believe that's the right decision. Now we must go back."

They walked back.

"The YPJ is more than an army for women," Komutan Rojda said. "The YPJ is a means to achieve equality for Kurdish women in particular, and Syrian women in general. Young women like you have thrived in war, the toughest test of all, and this is the first step to a society structured along similar lines to our army, where women can thrive on merit and not be held back by the capitalist patriarchy."

"I understand," Sarya said. "I've heard these things, but only when I was home on leave did it come to me. Then I understood.'

"When your mind was clear and fresh?"

"Yes."

They reached the team, now including Keya, waiting. "You must have elections for a new commander," Komutan Rojda said. "This is a matter for you alone," she said, before leaving.

They closed into a circle. "I stand to be elected as commander of Team Martyr Agir," Sarya said loudly and clearly.

There was silence as some kicked the ground and others looked away. Sarya wondered if listening to Komutan Rojda's advice was a mistake.

"I vote for Havel Sarya," Olan said. "I believe Sarya will be a good and effective commander."

"I vote for Havel Sarya," Soran said. "Sarya will be a good and effective commander, and she'll bring us along with her."

That left two; the most experienced.

"Congratulations Komutan Sarya," Keya said. "You earned this honour."

Barî clapped her on the back. "Congratulations Komutan Sarya," he said.

"Why don't you stand?" Sarya asked; totally confused.

"Because you saved Mina's life, when you applied first aid and then arranged for the supply van to take her to the base," Barî said. "Already you were our commander and Mina knew that. We knew that."

Sarya nodded her head slowly while she gathered her thoughts. "Thank you all, and I will try my best to justify your faith in me."

They broke up and Komutan Rojda came to them. "You have a decision?" she asked.

"We would like you to meet Komutan Sarya," Keya, the oldest, said.

Komutan Rojda kissed Sarya's cheeks. "Congratulations Komutan Sarya," she said. There's one other thing before I go. You need an extra member, and Havel Gulan Bashur has expressed a strong desire to fight on the front line of our battle against terrorism. Havel Gulan has worked in supplies and more recently in armaments, and that makes her familiar with your weapons. Over the next months we'll be taking and consolidating more villages like this one, which will be good preparation for Havel Gulan for when the time comes to defeat DAESH at Raqqah."

Sarya was pleased that her best friend was about to realise her dream to fight DAESH, and Komutan Rojda was right. These village by village battles would be excellent training.

"One thing before you go, Komutan Rojda," Sarya said. "Would you like to share tea with us, and our hosts here at Aalou?"

"What an excellent idea! Lead the way."

Havel Irem joined in, and Sarya was certain that Amena Hanano, the elder of the village, would be pleased and honoured to entertain the commander of the army which liberated her and her people from the cruelty of DAESH. While Sarya escorted her ultimate commander through the village, she thought that Mina and the rest of the team were right. Perhaps she was ready to be commander. She certainly felt like one.

* * *

Sarya came across Gulan staring across the plain while smoking a cigarette.

"Is it always that hard?" she asked.

"Sometimes it's harder," Sarya said, and then realised what she said. "I'm sorry. DAESH are always dug-in and we have to dig them out, and that's always hard. We have the option of calling airstrikes when we need them."

Gulan nodded while she drew on her cigarette, and then butted it. "You don't smoke?"

"I don't," Sarya said.

"Thank you for preparing me, and especially your target practice."

"You should thank Barî for his obstacle course of IEDs and trip wires."

"I will."

"Come with me."

"You seem so much a part of this," Gulan said.

"That will come to you in time. What's the saying? You have to crawl before you can walk, and soon these men will be your family."

Sarya and Gulan reached where the men played cards in a haze of smoke.

"Congratulations Gulan," Olan said. "You did well."

"Thank you Olan," Gulan said. "Thank you Barî for your training. It really helped."

"Olan's right," Barî said. "I've seen many first-timers, and you were good."

Sarya contemplated their team fighting for a Kurdish way of life after many decades of oppression, and fighting a greater threat from Arabs from places far away. That was the one constant in the history of her people, embedded into her soul.

"We drove out DAESH, thanks to the wonderful effort of you all, and the effort of our colleagues in this battle," Sarya said. "We Kurds have been fighting for our existence for a thousand years, and we'll be fighting for another thousand years I'm sure." Sarya put her fist over her heart and sang the first line of Ey Dijmin, and they all leapt to their feet and joined her, including Gulan, who surely looked at home amongst the veterans. Sarya loved her country, she loved her people, and she loved her family singing the Kurdish anthem in a village on the plains of Syria.

* * *

They sat in a circle for a tekmil.

"I called this tekmil for feedback on my role as commander, and for feedback for Gulan," Sarya said. "Who wants to start?"

"We know you already," Soran said. "Quietly determined to win the war against DAESH, and letting nothing stand in your way."

"But surely we all want to win the war against DAESH?"

"Some of us are happy to follow orders and play our part, and others are more determined."

Sarya contemplated that, and he was right. Soran did what he was told and did it well, and probably that's what he

216

was able to contribute. "There's a place for everybody in this world," Sarya said. "And a place for everybody in this war too."

"This is a new way for me," Keya said. "First we had Mina who was long-serving in the PYD before she came to us, and it was clear that Mina would be an able commander when we voted for her. Now we have Sarya, who's proven to me that women can volunteer like we volunteered, and are able to advance on merit. This battle with Komutan Sarya was different because she likes to get involved. But at the same time she kept everything and everyone coordinated for a good outcome, and you can't ask for more than that."

"Anyone else?" Sarya asked.

"I can't add anything more to what Soran and Keya said," Olan said.

"Thank you for your feedback. That feedback tells me to keep doing as I did. Now, we have a new member, Havel Gulan."

"I congratulated Gulan on the day," Olan said. "I know how hard it is first time, and Gulan did very well."

"Anyone else?"

"Gulan did an excellent job, being neither tentative nor reckless," Keya said. "I felt I could rely on her, no matter what was happening."

"Thank you for your feedback," Gulan said. "This type of meeting is useful because it can tell you where you can improve, but a tekmil also helps you if you're already performing well. With your feedback, I can build on what I did during this battle."

"Thank you all for your contributions," Sarya said. "Now, what are we going to do?

"Play cards and smoke cigarettes!" Barî said happily.

"Oh no; I shouldn't have asked," Sarya said, smiling. "Konkan?" she asked.

Barî shuffled his cards, while Sarya wondered what excuse she could offer to get out of the game after a few hands. Even patrolling was better than playing cards!

Chapter Twenty

Late October cold, the autumn of 2016; seeped through Vache's bones as he left his latest field hospital, a grand name for an improvised clinic in an abandoned village just out of Ayn Issa. He was lucky that he was well dressed for the conditions in warm trousers and a thick pullover. Around him soldiers in their thin, polyester camouflage rugged up as best they could, with windcheaters, parkas and sometimes gloves. Some stood around fires warming their hands. That build-up was bigger than Vache had ever seen. He didn't have to be told what it was about. What he saw were the preparations for the first stage of the push to Raqqah. That task had just become harder for the SDF. Already DAESH were losing the battle for Mosul in Iraq, and many DAESH fighters fled Mosul to defend their self-proclaimed capital of Raqqah.

The house next to the hospital was commandeered by the doctor and nurse, with space for other nurses when they came. Beyond was a house commandeered by a couple of Kurdish teams in the multi-ethnic Syrian Democratic Forces. Vache headed to his house, when he spotted someone familiar. He jogged to her.

"Sarya!" he exclaimed.

She turned and looked at him, before breaking into a big smile. "Vache," she replied. "Ma'a as-salaama," she greeted in Arabic.

"You can speak to me in Kurdish," Vache said in Kurdish.

She smiled brighter. "I will, although your accent!"

Vache shrugged his shoulders. "How are you, Komutan?" he asked with a smile.

"You heard? I'm tired but good. I've been fighting DAESH for what seems like half my life, but I believe more than ever that we're doing the right thing."

"If I didn't believe this isn't the right thing, I wouldn't be here."

"I know."

"Do you still want to be a doctor?"

"When this war's over, if it's ever over."

"Sarya!" Erna exclaimed, and came to the young commander and hugged her. "Congratulations," she said in Kurdish.

"You too," Sarya said while smiling brightly. "Come with me and I'll introduce you to our team."

Sarya led the way towards their house.

"Did you treat Komutan Mina when she was injured?" Sarya asked.

"We both did, and you did a good job with your first aid," Vache said.

"Thank you for saving her life."

"That's what we're here for."

In a former living room were a few mattresses and a few more blankets to sleep on. There Vache and Erna were introduced to Barî, Keya, Olan, Soran and Gulan, with Sarya telling her team that these are the people who saved Mina. Vache was kissed many times for that, and he was touched by their genuine gratitude. He was also quite surprised that a young woman, about twenty years old, was their commander. Then he thought he shouldn't have been surprised. The revolution started by Abdullah Öcalan, and shepherded by Rojda Felat and others, had been startlingly effective. Each according to his or her merits, regardless of race, religion or gender.

In another room, music played. Old music from his parent's time. The song ended and a more dynamic song came on. Vache knew what it was: Stevie Wonder's Master Blaster.

Erna grabbed Vache. "Come on," she said in Armenian. "This song's for dancing."

It wasn't really, but Vache had no choice. They went to a room with two soldiers, and Erna then danced to the slow, methodical beat while Vache imitated her steps, and the two soldiers gave their encouragement. Soon Sarya's team came to see what was happening, and they huddled around the doorway.

"Don't just look at us," Erna said in Kurdish. "Join in."

Some of the men danced, just as Sarya came into the room.

"You too," Erna said. "We women can show these men!"

Sarya joined in the dance, with all following Erna's steps to that Reggae classic.

"This is such a happy song!" Erna exclaimed.

The music was happy echoed by the words, which was an exhortation to put aside fighting and dance instead, which was apt. For that moment war was forgotten, and they were dancing Reggae. Until the end, and then another song came on.

"Oh no!" Erna exclaimed. "Play it again."

The comrade who'd been sitting and watching, fiddled with his mp3 player plugged into speakers, and Master Blaster returned. This time their dance went smoother, and for another five minutes war was forgotten. Everybody was happy at the end, although to be honest, those men and women were happy just to be alive and fighting, and even in love with each other, in a platonic sense. Vache often sensed their love, which was something he never expected in war. They lived as teams, fought as teams, and they felt platonic love as teams.

After the dancing ended, the gathering broke up. Vache took Sarya to one side.

"The end of this war's coming," he said. "When it's over, I can help you to become a doctor. But I don't have a home and you can't contact me."

Sarya took a notebook and pen from her pocket; frowned while writing, before tearing off a page. She gave it to Vache. "This is my father's name and address. He can tell you if I lived or not, and if I live he'll know where I am."

Vache felt like someone had hit him in the stomach. If she lived or not. How could a young woman deal with the thought of death at any moment?

"What is it?" she asked.

"How do you do it?" Vache asked.

"Who'll stop DAESH if I don't?" She looked into Vache's eyes. "Where are you from?"

"Originally Aleppo, and then Raqqah."

"After this, are you interested in living in Rojava? I know Erna is equal in your culture, but Rojava would be a good home for your children; especially if you have daughters. We need doctors and nurses in Rojava."

"I have to ask Erna of course, but you might be right. When this is over, Rojava might make a good home for us." Vache looked at the page from her notebook. "Amûdê."

"Yes."

She kissed his cheeks. "We'll meet again, I'm sure," she said.

"We will."

Vache watched Sarya join her team. He loved her, in a platonic sense.

* * *

Sarya used her binoculars to scan the countryside while Gulan stood beside with her rifle ready to protect them. Behind, the battle raged to take the village of Wasita. Sunday the 6th of November, 2016; and day one of Operation Wrath of Euphrates. Day one of the attack on Raqqah, and Sarya was sure DAESH would respond with all means at their disposal. Artillery, Technicals; even suicide attacks. She felt sure something would happen that day.

The slight rise gave Sarya a good view in all directions, but cold, damp, autumn weather hid tell-tale clouds of dust, which made spotting approaching vehicles more difficult. She kept alert; practice made her good at that, while she surveyed the flat countryside beneath a threatening, cloudy sky. She brought her binoculars around and in the distance something moved. Sarya adjusted her focus, and it was a vehicle alone.

"Car approaching," Sarya said. "Possibly a suicide car."

Sarya followed it closer and spotted the tell-tale grey of protective metal plate.

"Definitely a suicide car," Sarya said as she lowered her binoculars and grabbed the launcher. "Let's go."

Gulan slung her rifle over her shoulder and gathered the missiles at her feet. With the crude RPG-7; closer was better. They reached the road just as the evil grey car lumbered into view; its performance no doubt burdened by sheer weight of metal plate and explosive on board. There was nothing the suicide driver could do as Sarya loaded the RPG, stood, aimed, and gently squeezed the trigger. She watched the missile launch, and then accelerate to the target. Closer and closer, followed by a flash and explosion as the missile struck, and then a second, massive explosion as the suicide car was consumed by its payload. Sarya grinned. She wasn't trained to use an RPG-7, but had achieved good successes despite that.

DAESH for all their money, manpower and resources, and their initial victories against the Iraqi army and Assad's army, were now desperate. Only in desperation would a combatant rely on suicide attacks.

"I don't believe we'll have more suicide attacks," Sarya said to Gulan while they walked back to the rise. "I must catch up on the others, so I'll send someone out to protect you. If you see an enemy vehicle; use the launcher."

Gulan nodded, and with a few practice shots she'd proven to be proficient with the RPG.

Sarya kept her head low while she sprinted to the village proper, where she found her team pinned down by a sniper. They were protected by a low wall, where they shot a few rounds before ducking as carefully aimed bullets thudded into the house behind them. There was one possibility, although Sarya had never used it that way before.

"Olan," she said. "Come with me."

Sarya led the way to Gulan, and got Olan to grab a few missiles while she retrieved the launcher. At the village she instructed Olan to give her covering fire for a moment. He stood and shot while Sarya put her head just above the wall to see the only place the sniper could be. Then they both ducked. Sarya loaded the RPG while she asked them all to give her covering fire. They stood and shot, while Sarya launched a missile at the second storey window of a house about 100 metres away. She ducked and everybody ducked, followed by an explosion. No sniper fire. Sarya grinned again.

Time for reality. "Olan," Sarya said. "Take the RPG to Gulan, and protect her while she's searching for suicide cars or Technicals. Now that the sniper's gone, the rest of us can advance."

"We need proper rockets," Barî grumbled.

"I know," Sarya said. "Maybe one day."

They advanced through the village, to be stopped by two men with typical DAESH beards. A quick exchange in Arabic, and those men surrendered. They were searched for weapons and suicide explosives, before being disabled with cable ties at wrists and ankles. Onward past the body of a

DAESH terrorist, with just sporadic shooting in the background. Sarya came to Hedar and Nefel, conversing.

"Ah Sarya," Hedar said with a big smile. "You've been blowing things up again!"

Sarya smiled brightly. "We blew-up a sniper, a suicide car, and we have two DAESH terrorists who surrendered," Sarya said. "Is anyone left fighting on their side?"

He shook his head. "No. I'll radio victory through, and ask for a vehicle to pick up the prisoners."

"This was easy, Hedar."

"They've totally lost the initiative."

Sarya looked around the damaged village, and expected inhabitants to return in the next day or so. They from the SDF would wait there at Wasita, until others took villages closer to Raqqah. Then with a new front line, they could advance. In the meantime the PYD would help villagers to elect commune and neighbourhood representatives. The SDF liberated villagers from DAESH, and opened the door not to Kurdish rule; but to self-rule of Arab, Kurd, Assyrian, Armenian, Shia, Sunni and Christian; all together. But for now, the SDF had a job to do.

"How do you want to patrol?" Sarya asked.

"We'll do from now through tonight; you can do tomorrow from dawn, and us tomorrow afternoon, and then you can do night and so on.

"We'll find somewhere to camp." Sarya faced her team. "Soran; can you fetch Olan and Gulan and meet us here?"

He jogged off, and shortly after, Olan and Gulan returned carrying the RPG and missiles. From there they found an empty shop with the roller door blown in, and seconded that until owners returned, if they returned. Sarya sat on the floor cross-legged, and knew anything she said would be trite. No, not at all.

"This was day one of the battle to seize the capital city of DAESH!" she proudly announced.

They all cheered loudly.

Sarya pondered how many villages they'd taken, and how many would come over the next months. At least they were at the beginning of the end.

* * *

Sarya peered through a sniping hole in their sandbag wall. After 19 days of SDF advances, DAESH were fighting back at Qaltah. But they were out of range for all but the PK.

"Stop shooting!" Sarya shouted, but Gulan and Soran didn't hear her. Keeping low, Sarya went to them and they stopped.

"Olan," Sarya said. "Pick them out as best you can. Gulan; feed the belt."

Gulan went to the PK and guided the ammunition belt, which allowed Olan to pivot the gun on its tripod without the belt jamming. Olan continued firing one shot at a time, and surprisingly pinning DAESH down. But those 20 or more terrorists would eventually advance on a team of six; with another 10 or 20 terrorists near the pumping station, facing Hedar's team of six. While Sarya used her binoculars, she pondered what those men in black would do if they overran the village. She knew they would do something terrible; like when they burned that poor Jordanian pilot to death. For sure those terrorists would kill every SDF soldier they captured, in the most barbaric way possible. *Gulan and she?* Muslim men couldn't take Muslim women as sex slaves; but Sarya knew something sexual would happen to Gulan and she. Those barbarians would be particularly cruel to two woman soldiers. There was only one chance.

Sarya went to ever reliable Keya. "I'm arranging for more troops," she said. "If they advance; you know what to do."

He nodded, while Sarya got close to Gulan.

"Do you have your grenades?" Sarya shouted in her ear.

Gulan nodded.

"If worst comes to worst," Sarya said. "Use one to avoid being captured."

Gulan nodded again, while Sarya felt her grenades in her flak jacket pockets. It was better to be a martyr than to suffer the brutalities DAESH would inflict on her.

Keeping low; Sarya sprinted to the centre of Qaltah, where she found Hedar.

"I'm radioing for backup," she said.

He looked hurt.

"We're outnumbered more than three to one," Sarya said. "We must even that up."

"Alright," he agreed.

Sarya took her radio and pressed transmit. "Komutan Sarya Goran from Team Martyr Agir. We're under attack at Qaltah by a larger DAESH force, and we urgently need reinforcements. At least ten, but twenty would be better."

They confirmed her request, and Sarya hoped reinforcements would arrive before DAESH attacked. Sarya contemplated the village taken five day's before. She could do a DAESH, and without air support that could work. If necessary, they could fall back from the perimeter wall and use houses facing the DAESH advance, and that would buy precious time. Keeping low she returned to the sandbag wall, where two DAESH Technicals had rolled into position. Soon DAESH would advance under covering fire, and probably protected by rockets.

Sarya grabbed the RPG and loaded a missile, to stand and shoot the closest Technical. She missed. She loaded again, and hit it. Sarya loaded another missile, stood, just as the entire contingent of DAESH terrorists advanced into the open. A rocket round whizzed past and exploded somewhere behind, while DAESH ran across open ground; something they rarely did, and as they closed into range her people opened fire. Sarya took her own rifle and joined in, but terrorist casualties didn't stop them. For once they were behaving like soldiers. Her team kept firing, the PK continued to spray lead, but still DAESH advanced accompanied by covering fire from the surviving Technical. Sarya pictured DAESH scaling the sandbag wall, soon.

Sarya told Barî, Keya and Soran to shoot from houses in the village, and immediately they left. After a few moments they were shooting once more, but protected by more robust defences.

Sarya told Soran and Gulan to take the PK into a house in the village, and they set to carrying it as it was. Sarya carried the RPG, and a few minutes later Sarya was in another house with Gulan and Olan, while inhabitants fled.

DAESH reached the sandbag wall, where they were under fire from houses ten metres further away. DAESH shot and their team shot back, while the PK had an impact on men relatively exposed. Fire from the DAESH Technical mostly hit walls of houses. Every now and then a bullet would ping inside, while Sarya sniped from a window just along from Olan and Gulan, and she got a terrorist carrying an RPG. That was the end of DAESH rocket fire.

Then Sarya heard shooting from the far side of the village towards the pumping station. The second DAESH force was advancing on Hedar's team. Some terrorists scaled the sandbag wall and entered the village proper, while still under fire. They didn't run away so Sarya contemplated her options. But she had no options. If their team didn't stop DAESH they would be captured and killed in the cruellest ways possible, with those killings filmed and posted on the internet. Sarya had to do something to save them, but she didn't know what.

Rifle fire came from their left aimed towards DAESH, and reinforcements had arrived! Sarya breathed a sigh of relief and felt tension abate from her body. She sniped along with their team and their reinforcements, to force DAESH back over the wall, and soon out of range of their Kalashnikovs. Olan's fire drove them further away, and he was doing a sterling job.

Relative silence except for Olan on single-shot once more. Sarya went to their reinforcements, to meet Komutan Beng.

"Thank you for that," she said. "Are there reinforcements for the other team?"

"Yes there are."

"You should go there regardless, and if we need you I'll radio."

He took his men and one woman away, while Sarya used her binoculars to view terrorists who didn't seem to know what to do next. The Technical drove away while men followed on foot, and it seemed they were headed towards the pumping station. Now, she couldn't abandon the other front. She went to the house.

"Gulan," she said. "Can you go to the battle for the pumping station, and if they need us then tell me?"

"Yes Sarya," Gulan said, before leaving the room. Sarya moved to sit beside Olan amongst a thousand spent cartridge cases, and watch out the window.

"You did a great job, as always," she said.

"Thanks," Olan replied.

"Do you remember our first battle together?"

"That seems like a lifetime ago."

"This will be over one day.'

"I know."

Rifle fire echoed as the battle for the pumping station continued, but Gulan didn't return so that must have been under control. Eventually that rifle fire faded to just the odd shot, and Gulan came into the room.

"DAESH have retreated out of range, so it's over for now," Gulan said. "Hedar said he will patrol that side, and he suggested we patrol this side and see what happens."

Sarya nodded, and resumed her gaze across the damp but firm, bare earth field. At that moment she felt tired. Their team was wonderful and everyone did exactly as they should, but success or failure was on her shoulders. Sarya sighed and got to her feet. It was time to organise who would patrol with who, for how long, while the rest had a break for food and water.

Chapter Twenty One

After a few weeks break, airstrikes returned more intensely than ever, but this time mostly at night at targets beyond the outskirts in Raqqah. It was eerie to lie in bed and listen to the roar of jet aircraft and explosions, but explosions not so close to be dangerous. Adnan had seen many movies of war, where air raids were repelled by fighter aircraft and anti-aircraft fire. All DAESH had were snipers and suicide vests, while Coalition aircraft flew totally unmolested. For those pilots, bombing Raqqah must have been more like a training exercise than war.

Eventually after a few hours sleep, the alarm on Adnan's phone sprang into life. Wearily he got out of bed and went to the bathroom, where he had a leak and pressed the button to flush, which happened but the cistern didn't refill. Then he turned the taps on the shower, but nothing happened. He turned them all the way, and still nothing.

"Adnan," Ranim called from the kitchen, and he went to her.

"There's no water," she said.

Adnan rubbed his dirty hair. "They've blown up the water pumping station," he said.

"Why?"

Adnan shrugged his shoulders. That didn't make sense at all. "I'll dress and get some water from the well," he said, before realising something. "We can't operate a cafe without water."

Ranim put her hands to her mouth.

"It's alright my love," Adnan said. "Raqqah's dying, but it'll be over soon. I'll dress."

After dressing in his usual black shirt, black track-suit trousers with black trainers, Adnan took the two plastic jugs Ranim gave him to the well, where there was already a crowd for water. Adnan waited his turn before pumping the handle to fill the two, four-litre jugs. Then he headed home to sparingly wash his face at least, before Ranim served breakfast of bread with honey, and some tea.

Now what? "I'll visit Papa at home and we'll put the cafe to rest."

Adnan spent a few hours with his parents working out financial plans. Adnan had a bit over 300 dollars, mostly earned from his work with Abdul and then changed with a money dealer after the Syrian pound started to collapse in value, while his parents had a bit more than that. Adnan decided to put 100 dollars aside for emergencies, and be even more careful with what was left. Clearly invasion was coming soon, and then what? Four months? His money wasn't enough, especially given the high price of food, but they would have to do the best with what they had.

Adnan returned home to find Ranim entertaining Hardi and his wife Marla. Adnan hugged his best friend before kissing Marla on her cheeks. They sat in the living room.

"What brings you around my friend?" Adnan asked.

"I'm out of work because there's no water," Hardi said. "I knew you would be the same."

"Have you got enough to get by?"

"I hope so. And you?"

"I hope so."

"Have you heard about the damage?" Hardi asked.

"Obviously the water pumping station."

"Also all bridges, especially to the south. Now's a good time to leave, but DAESH shoot anyone on sight, and especially crossing by boat. So roads are patrolled, fields are mined, and boats are dangerous."

"People are leaving."

"And some are dying when they leave."

"Well then we stay," Adnan said. "Now that you're both here; let's make the most of this forced unemployment."

"Music, television, radio, internet...."

Adnan laughed. "In your dreams. This is the Seventh Century, and surely they had cards."

"Surely they did."

Adnan went to the bedroom to fetch his deck of cards for a game of forty-one. A game for four people, which was an ideal way to pass a lazy day in Raqqah.

Rain pattered on the temporary canvas roof above their heads, while drips splashed onto the concrete floor from a few leaks. Inside the part-ruined house was warm, dry and smoky, while Sarya pondered her hand. Soran stood to one side; using his binoculars to scan the fertile plain being nourished by spring rains, while outside Gulan patrolled; partly protected from the weather by a waterproof parka. Sarya put down a Kiçek and picked up a Shahip in its place, which wasn't what she wanted. She frowned, and put her hand down.

"Ah," Barî said, smiling brightly. "You lose again."

Indeed Sarya had lost another two pounds.

The hand of konkan went on with Barî taking the pot, at least temporarily. Sarya pondered how many hundreds of generations had welcomed spring rain on these plains, before the heat and dryness of summer. She wondered how many generations relied on their crops for food and income. She wondered how long before these farmers, and the shopkeepers and traders they supported, would get back to a normal life. That gave her an idea.

"Betting on cards is one thing," Sarya said. "Let's bet on something useful."

"That's only because you've been losing," Barî gloated.

"No," Sarya said defensively. "We all want this to be over and to be home once more, so let's work this out."

"You have an advantage," Keya said.

"I don't," Sarya said. "We haven't yet been briefed, so all I know is where we started, where we are now, and where Raqqah is. I'll show you."

Sarya grabbed the tablet computer and brought up the big map. She showed each village including this village of Kabash Gharbi, and then Raqqah.

"Each of us chooses how long it will take to get to and defeat Raqqah. Remember it's a big city of two-hundred and twenty thousand, and it's their capital so they'll defend it strongly. Ten pounds each, and a real bet where we don't hand the money back at the end."

"Alright," Barî said. "You start."

Sarya pondered the map. It was April 17, 2017; and she guessed it would take a bit less than two months to get to Raqqah. Then what? Much of the SDF would be involved, and Coalition aircraft. Four months to take Raqqah? "Six months," Sarya said. "October seventeen."

"It won't take that long," Keya said. "Four months. Two months to Raqqah, and two months to take Raqqah."

"It's a big city," Sarya said.

"But look at al-Shaddadah. Americans said that would take six weeks, and we did it in three days!"

"But al-Shaddadah has only fifteen thousand people. That's smaller than my city of Amûdê."

"Four months," Keya repeated.

"Alright," Sarya said. "Barî?" she asked.

He rubbed his chin. "This is going to be hard," he said, ever the optimist. "Nine months."

"Are you sure?"

"You said it's a big city and DAESH will fight to the end, so two months to Raqqah and seven months to take the city."

"Alright. Olan?"

"Five months."

Soran?"

He came to the tablet computer, while Olan went to use the binoculars to scan the plain. Soran frowned. "Seven months."

Gulan came into their shelter dripping with water. She took off the wet parka and put it to one side, along with her rifle. Sarya quickly explained their bet, and went through the villages they'd taken, where they where, and where Raqqah was.

Gulan looked hard at the map. "Six months," she said.

"Sarya already said six months," Olan said.

"That's alright," Sarya said. "If we both win, we'll split the money." Sarya stood. "Now it's my turn to patrol," she said, while she put the tablet away and pulled on the wet parka.

"Do you think they'll attempt to retake this village in this weather?" Olan asked.

"This is a bad day for fighting," Sarya said. "If I was losing; I would pick a day when battle was least expected. That way you might catch your enemy off guard."

"Here's your money back," Barî said, and Sarya put out her hand for her six pounds. She grabbed her rifle, went to the doorway without a front door, pulled the hood over her hair, and stepped into the rain. It was going to be a long four hours.

Chapter Twenty Two

Early on a warm, sunny morning, they were in the back of one of three utilities escorted by an armoured personnel carrier made from sheet steel welded onto a Toyota Landcruiser chassis, approaching the northern outskirts of Raqqah. June six, 2017; and day one of the Battle of Raqqah. The city outskirts surprised Sarya, being simple houses and commercial buildings made of concrete block, in a dry, dusty landscape. They could have been in her city of Amûdê and not approaching a big city. The convoy stopped, and they all jumped down to proceed on foot, while looking for mines or IEDs. Her team advanced holding rifles at the ready, while their accompanying Arab soldiers walked with rifles casually slung over shoulders. Sarya also slung her rifle because she carried the tablet computer, but she was alert for danger after taking countless villages, where initial peace and calm could be broken in a moment by snipers or full-scale attacks. The Arabs, a necessary part of the SDF, didn't have that experience, and it showed.

As they reached the first buildings on that road, Sarya was ever more alert for IEDs, but saw none. They entered Raqqah proper, amongst the first SDF to do so, where Sarya saw no damage despite many airstrikes the day before. Those targets must have been further to the south. Other SDF were tasked to take a Syrian army base to the east, while Sarya had instructions to advance about 300 metres and then consolidate. While being alert she was also excited; this was the beginning of the end of DAESH. She was actually inside their capital, where a building had 'Islamic State' painted in black in Arabic, black standards, their battle flag, were painted on other buildings, while a DAESH flag flew from a roof. An Arab man in black robes and a white guttrah came out to greet them, so Sarya instructed Barî and Olan to intercept him. They discreetly but firmly grabbed his robes and searched for suicide explosives, before kissing his cheeks in greeting, while Gulan and Soran stood back with their rifles trained. Surprisingly, he really was just a resident greeting the liberating army!

Spasmodic rifle fire carried from where other teams advanced in parallel, but that sector of the Mashlab district was as quiet as could be. Sarya checked her tablet and moved on towards the building designated as their command post. They entered a commercial sector along with the Arab teams, and continued to walk forward. Sarya reached the designated building not far short of a multi-lane road, and waited while their Arab colleagues negotiated use of that warehouse. It was actually two buildings: with a single-storey building and a double-story complex next door.

Successfully arranged, they entered through a loading dock with very few goods on pallets, and probably business had dried up under the rule of DAESH. Sarya took their team to the two-storey complex and upstairs, and then up to the roof where she posted lookouts to all four corners. There they scanned, but all was still and quiet. That was good, because any DAESH advance would stand out. Nothing of note, except for an SDF van unloading next door. Sarya went downstairs and gathered an armful of water bottles, and brought them to her grateful comrades. Sarya drank while she watched through her binoculars, and saw movement far in the distance. Car-sized, dark and lumbering, and already a suicide car!

They had no defence other than the rifles they carried, but that didn't matter. Sarya called to evacuate the building, and ran down the stairs to the ground floor and into next door. She shouted in Arabic that a suicide car was coming, before running to find a rear exit. Indeed there was a door, but it was locked. Sarya shot at the lock before pushing that door open. They ran into a rear yard towards the street behind, just as a massive explosion shattered the peace and calm. The sheer bulk of the building protected them from the blast, but the Arabs weren't around.

Sarya went inside the smoky building with her trainers crunching on shards of glass. The building was structurally intact, but many Arab soldiers were hurt after the blast blew out windows and doors. Their team dispensed first aid while Sarya radioed for ambulances. She then went outside, but all she saw was scorched bitumen, which was good. The supply van must have departed before the suicide car arrived. Of the suicide car there was no trace.

There Sarya waited for ambulance vans to take the first casualties of the Battle of Raqqah for treatment. She kept her rifle ready, because someone radioed DAESH about what was going on. Two white vans arrived; where two drivers, two nurses and their team helped the seven injured men into those vans. They weren't so badly injured; mostly cut from broken glass. Sarya scanned the street for signs of another attack, but all was quiet. She asked their team to stay outside and check, while she went upstairs to retrieve her tablet.

On the roof Sarya radioed a report and suggested they find a different command post, because of the damage and the possibility of another attack. She was given coordinates, so went downstairs to gather their team, which was all there was left of that part the forward advance. Further along the next street was a double-storey building. There she conversed in Arabic with the manager, and arranged use of his building for a time. Their team went upstairs to the roof and posted lookouts once more, to wait for comrades to arrive.

* * *

Airstrikes day and night and artillery shelling too, yet Adnan hadn't seen troops on the ground; just the ongoing destruction of Raqqah. More and more buildings were damaged or reduced to rubble, while clouds of dirt and dust hung over the city. DAESH militants occupied buildings in various parts of the city, probably in preparation for the assault by Kurdish forces, surely to come soon. There were lesser militants than before, as those less fanatical left DAESH. Adnan pictured them discarding their rifles, shaving their beards, changing their clothes, and boarding trucks with those fortunate enough to pay a bribe. There they would be welcomed by the United Nations, to be given accommodation and meals as reward for destroying Syria.

Raqqah ground ever more to a halt as little, or even no produce entered the city. Food was in short supply and very expensive, and mostly they made do with bread baked by Ranim from wheat and oil, and rice; which was all they could afford. One saving grace was their landlord agreed to accept credit for the rental of their apartment. Adnan still had his 100 dollars in a glass bottle hidden in a cupboard, as a last resort. He bought food using the balance of his cash while hoping it would last. Each day he went to the well to fetch a couple of jugs of water, and hoped DAESH wouldn't shoot him on the way. Safe in their apartment felt like sanctuary. Sanctuary, until he heard knocking on the door. Adnan opened that door to see his friend Hardi, who looked peculiar. Pale with his eyes big and yet darting, and just looking peculiar.

"You have to come with me," Hardi said.

"Why?" Adnan asked.

"Just come."

Adnan did, down the staircase, outside where artillery boomed and missiles exploded ever closer. Definitely closer. They went around the corner, along a street, and around another corner. That was a route Adnan walked many times over past years, and he felt his heart racing faster and faster. *No, it couldn't be.* Hardi walked briskly, but not fast enough. They rounded the final corner, where the building was collapsed into rubble. Hardi grabbed Adnan's arm hard.

"There's nothing you can do," he said.

"What?" Adnan exclaimed.

"There's nothing we can do."

"All of them?" Adnan asked, while not believing such a tragedy could be true.

"I'm afraid so."

Hardi walked slowly to several shapes covered in white sheets. Victims of the airstrike.

"I must see," Adnan said.

Hardi knelt and turned over the ends of three sheets. There was Mama, Papa and Lina; cut down in her prime. Adnan stared at that while totally lost for words or action. He felt he should have been shocked or angry or even outraged, but he felt strangely numb.

"We have to arrange their funerals," Hardi said.

"Yes," Adnan said, but too blank to think that through.

"We can't leave them in the street like this, so I'll arrange burial for tomorrow morning."

"Where?" Adnan asked; knowing cemeteries were no longer accessible.

"Seven Nisan Park. Who do you want to attend?"

"There's so many," Adnan said while thinking about uncles, aunts and cousins.

"This is dangerous and we have to be realistic. Who are the minimum?"

Adnan knew straight away. "Ranim and her family."

"You speak with them, and I'll arrange this burial."

"Yes, yes," Adnan said, before and grabbing Hardi's arm. "Thank you for this."

"There's nothing to thank me for, because if roles were reversed, you'd do the same for me."

Adnan nodded while he contemplated that, and Hardi was right. Without hesitation.

"You and Ranim should wash and re-shroud," Hardi said.

"We will."

"I'll leave you," Hardi said. "I'm terribly sorry for your loss."

"Thank you dear friend."

Hardi left while Adnan stared at those sheets. He couldn't believe his family was gone; along with neighbours he grew up with. Never again would he see his sensible and practical Papa, who in his own quiet way, devoted his life to his wife and his children. Never again would he see his loving Mama, whose reason for existence was her family, and especially her children. And never again would he see Lina, who was his best friend as much as she was his sister, and who he loved dearly. Without his love for Lina, Adnan would never have been able to love Ranim so much. Adnan felt his eyes go moist, and he felt terribly, terribly sad. His ruined home spilled onto the road, and he wondered why Kurds and Americans blew it up. Was it a DAESH target? Would they destroy a building for one, possible DAESH target?

Adnan headed home to find Ranim pacing the living room. Their eyes met and he knew she knew.

"I'm sorry," she said.

Adnan hugged her. "I'll miss them," he said, but those words didn't explain how he really felt. He felt hollow inside; like someone had taken away his soul.

"I feel like I've lost my family."

Adnan wanted to ask 'will this ever end?' but he knew the answer. Yes it would, but only after many more tragedies.

"We have to wash and re-shroud, while Hardi arranges a funeral for tomorrow," Adnan said. "I want your family to attend, because they're my family too."

Ranim nodded her head. "I'll dress to go out."

She left the room, and returned a few moments later in black. Adnan grabbed one of their water jugs along with a cloth, and they headed out the door.

* * *

Seven Nisan Park was turned into a cemetery, for victims of airstrikes and artillery, and of course for those who died from natural causes. There, decent men offered their services at modest prices, given the economic situation of many who lost their loved ones. Abdi, Sarina and Lina Richie were laid to rest, taken from this world too soon, because of factors outside everyone's control. If DAESH hadn't behaved as they did, and if the Kurds and Americans hadn't been so reckless, then none of that would have happened. But it did, and to preserve the legacy of his family he loved, Adnan knew he must ensure their deaths weren't in vain.

Ranim's wonderful family were deeply shocked and very supportive, especially for Ranim who lost the family she loved. Only her eyes were visible and they were red with silent crying. Adnan felt on the verge of tears but he fought them back, for the duration of the service at least. When Papa Fakhri, Mama Fakhri, Saami and Hardi left, he didn't fight that anymore. Tears overflowed and he felt better. Ranim stared at those graves, but she seemed to sense Adnan's grief because she took his hand, and that felt better still. Adnan stared at those graves too, with tears running down his cheeks while the sound of war played in the background. Explosions particularly; with more tragedy. They had to get away before they became victims.

"They were good people, and now they've gone peacefully to a better place," Ranim said quietly.

Adnan agreed. If any on earth were good enough to go peacefully; they were. He took one last look. "We'll meet again one day," Adnan said, and he was sure they would. Adnan took a big, deep breath, and led Ranim out of the park turned cemetery. As much as he wanted to devote his time to grief, that wasn't possible. They had to get away, to preserve the legacy of his family. Perhaps at night they could get past DAESH guarding roads leading out of Raqqah, but he wondered if he should he take Ranim's family into his confidence and risk things going badly for them. They reached their apartment building, where Adnan wearily climbed stairs to a home which felt strangely like a prison.

"We must leave Raqqah," he said.

"When?" Ranim asked.

"Tonight."

"What about my family?"

"I don't know. This is dangerous and they could get hurt."

She paced the room; clearly deep in thought. "It won't come to me," she said.

"Nor me. If it doesn't come easily then I think we shouldn't tell them."

"I think you're right, although it would be terrible if...."

"It would be terrible the other way."

She nodded her head. "Have you thought about what to do?" she asked.

"After dark, and then head north, because bridges to the south are destroyed. I've got that money and I hope it's enough."

"We'll pack what we can carry, and I'll make some bread for the journey, and we'll take drink bottles of water. I'll cook some bread now."

"I'll fetch some water."

That June day passed too slowly; while they waited for the sun to eventually set. Eventually the evening darkened, and with backpacks slung in place, they locked their door and headed into the street. Darkness was their friend, because they may be able to get away without being noticed. Despite the late hour airstrikes continued. Raqqah had gone from being slaughtered silently, to being completely destroyed. Which was worse? Barbarity, cruelty and random executions for little reason, or this? At least war in Raqqah would soon come to an end, because DAESH couldn't hold off a large army and multiple airforces for more than a few months, if that.

They walked those first blocks where many buildings were damaged, while some were destroyed with rubble spilling onto roads. But little moved on that street at that time of evening.

"What are you two up to?" an accented voice asked.

Adnan turned around to see a bearded, DAESH militant with his rifle over his shoulder. To be confronted while carrying bags at night was dangerous, and they could be killed for that. But Adnan felt strangely calm; because he was used to death all around him.

"Our parents were killed," Ranim said.

"Brother and sister?"

"Husband and wife. My husband's parents, who were good to me."

"And you decided to leave?"

"Yes," she said quietly. "We have some money."

"I'm not interested in money."

"What are you interested in?" Ranim asked provocatively, while loosening her niqab to reveal her face. Adnan was partly shocked, but then wondered if that sacrifice could save their lives.

"I'm not interested in another man's wife." He came close to them. "You are beautiful though, and it would be a shame to spoil your beauty." He lit a cigarette and drew on it. "I think you should go home and stay there. Perhaps you're in shock from your loss, caused by barbaric Kurds and Americans."

"It has been a shock," Adnan said. "I haven't been thinking clearly since then."

"That's solved then."

Adnan took Ranim's hand, and led her towards their apartment which was like a prison. There they would stay, and hope DAESH didn't turn their building into an airstrike target.

Chapter Twenty Three

Men and a few women filed out of the semi-ruined building while Sarya led their team to Clara. Clara showed their objective on her tablet computer. Sarya memorised the route about 400 metres away, and headed downstairs and outside.

Every day brought more airstrikes and more destruction, with rubble and concrete dust everywhere. Every single building in Raqqah was damaged, from blown-out windows to structures nearly destroyed. Sarya trudged through dust and around piles of rubble, while holding her rifle firmly and scanning for IEDs and mines, and listening for drones. Bodies lay in the streets: mostly unarmed civilians shot by DAESH but a few DAESH terrorists as well. The stench of rotting corpses never went away. The smell of concrete dust was just as pervasive, while the roar of a jet and the crack of a missile explosion somewhere in the distance, added more dust and rubble to the ruins of Raqqah.

They reached a cross-street where everyone knew to stop. Sarya peered around the corner to scan a street which was continuous, which meant less chance of being caught by a sniper. Sarya sprinted across the gap, heart racing from stress and not exertion, and having made it across unharmed the rest of the team then ran across that open ground.

Onwards they walked, and just after another missile strike in the distance, she heard that familiar buzz.

"Drone!" she shouted, before looking for cover. But there was no cover and they were terrible things to shoot down. Sarya aimed and shot, but missed as always. They all shot and all missed, while the drone circled with its deadly payload of a grenade. The operator of that drone was somewhere around; ready to kill them while safe in his cavern. Always DAESH terrorists stayed indoors; a few floors up from street level in an apartment, and always protected by booby-traps and human shields. The team kept shooting and suddenly the drone plunged to earth. Somebody shot it although Sarya didn't know how. In anger she wanted to kick the wreckage but didn't; instead she looked up at the multi-storey apartment buildings lining that street, and seemingly every street in Raqqah. *Why didn't they come out and fight, the cowards?*

Sarya took a deep breath to calm her anger, and headed towards the next intersection. There she stopped, and carefully looked both ways where her heart fell. It was a dead-end and surely a trap. She eased out from behind the building on the corner just as bullets thudded past from a heavy machine gun somewhere nearby, and she pulled back. Sarya moved out and fired several rounds while trying to get a fix on the machine gun, but couldn't locate it.

She beckoned Soran, Barî and Keya to come out and shoot, which they did in turns while Sarya searched for their tormentor. She saw his muzzle flash at the end of that street on the third floor, and within range.

"Give me cover," Sarya asked while she fitted a replacement magazine, and they did that while she took her stance to snipe at the broken window, for all the good that did. It was easy to take that shot 100 metres away, except under relentless machine gun fire. Cover was cover, but you had to rush your shot and that made it difficult.

"Get back!" Sarya shouted, and they retreated. "Gulan; try the RPG while we cover you. Did you see where he is?"

"I saw his muzzle flash," Gulan said while she lowered the RPG. She dropped her heavy backpack to the ground and unbuckled the cover. Gulan fed a missile into the RPG before hoisting it onto her shoulder. Sarya nodded, and Gulan stepped from safety to kneel in the cross-street, while Sarya, Soran, Barî and Keya stood behind to shoot at the sniper. Bullets from the machine gun cracked all around, whizzed past their bodies, and even kicked up dust near their feet. Seconds seemed like hours before the usual boom and whoosh, and then they sprinted to safety just as the missile exploded against their target. Already Gulan loaded another missile, before stepping into the rain of lead once more, while Sarya, Soran, Barî and Keya provided cover once more. Again they retreated. Sarya peered around the corner to see the apartment quite damaged by RPG missiles, but not enough to stop the terrorist. She wondered; but to take out the building would kill any human shields. Despite the risk, she had no choice.

"Once more," Sarya said, and Gulan nodded. Once more they stepped into remorseless machine gun fire, and once more Gulan knelt and fired a missile at their tormentor. Once more they retreated, and once more Sarya peered around the corner to see the apartment even more damaged, but the machine gunner was still able to operate. That was hopeless.

"I'll call a strike," Sarya said, and Gulan nodded.

Sarya pulled her new smartphone out of her flak jacket pocket to locate that street and the building which held that sniper, to identify the coordinates. She radioed those coordinates to the operator, who would translate to English and radio the Coalition, who would then radio a pilot in one of the many jets endlessly circulating the Raqqah airspace.

Meanwhile, Sarya leaned against a wall and waited. Any human shields the DAESH terrorist had accumulated were done for, but the team had done all that was possible. A jet closed, their jet, followed by an explosion where yet another Raqqah building was blown-up. Sarya peered around the corner to see they got the right one, which was great news. Just to be sure she ran across the intersection, and no machine gun fire. The rest of the team sprinted across that intersection, and then they trudged towards their objective which was to take a building about 100 metres further on.

That would become part of the new front line as other teams advanced in parallel that day, although in a maze of streets and multi-storey buildings, the concept of a 'front line' was impossible to picture on the ground. Nonetheless they were gradually squeezing DAESH from east, west and south towards the north.

Onwards they advanced; searching and scanning for booby traps of all types, until the third intersection and the building which was their objective. The ground floor consisted of what was once Cafe Hamid, but a blown-in roller door showed a darkened cavern of wrecked tables and chairs, and a bench covered in filth. Beside that was a doorway, door long gone, leading to a staircase and apartments above. Rifle at the ready, Sarya stepped into the relative gloom of the small entrance lobby, and there she stopped until her eyes adjusted to the darkness.

"We'll wait here for a few moments," Sarya said, and they nodded in agreement. They knew her routine. "Now we go," Sarya said, and led their team up dirty, dusty stairs. Helped by light filtering through dirty windows, Sarya's eyes probed for trip wires and IEDS as she climbed around and around flights of stairs in the three-storey building. Higher and higher, beyond the top floor to a doorway which led to the roof. There Sarya stopped.

"Barî and Keya," Sarya said, before easing the door open.

Rifles at the ready; they raced through the doorway and onto the roof, and all was silence.

"It's clear," Keya said. Sarya followed Olan onto the roof, while the rest came in turn and spread to all four corners. There they would stay until relieved, while Sarya surveyed the near vicinity. There were two, taller apartment buildings both about 100 metres away, which overlooked that roof. She took her binoculars and checked each building thoroughly, but saw nothing out of the ordinary. While the team scanned street level she kept her gaze on those two buildings.

"Down there," Gulan said.

Sarya went to the edge of the roof, where she saw children dressed in black; holding rifles while they filed into the doorway beside the cafe. *Goh!*

"They'll come onto the roof and we need to deal with them," Sarya said flatly.

"But they're children!" Gulan exclaimed.

"I know; but they've got rifles and they've been trained, and they'll kill us if we don't deal with them!"

"You say deal when you mean kill."

"I'm hoping under fire or with a few casualties, they'll surrender. So we deal with them, and if necessary we kill them before they kill us."

"Sarya's right," Keya said firmly.

"Olan," Sarya said; wanting to give those boys a chance to surrender. "Just use the PK on single-shot. Everybody get ready. When they come through that doorway, I'll talk with them first."

Their team gathered several metres from the open door with rifles aimed. Sarya stood in the centre, but to one side with her rifle aimed. The first figure in black emerged, and Sarya shot at the timber door hanging open beside him. The boy aged about 10 and wearing a DAESH windcheater, lifted his rifle.

"Surrender!" Sarya shouted in Arabic. "You don't have a chance."

He brought his rifle around in what seemed like slow motion.

"Surrender!" Keya bellowed in Arabic. "Surrender or we'll kill you."

"Allahu akbar!" the boy shouted in a high-pitched voice as he moved further onto the roof, and other boys came from behind.

Sarya sighted the first boy; squeezed her trigger, and he fell. Rapid rifle fire came from their team, and those boys emerging from the stairwell didn't stand a chance. Some boys backed away.

"Stop, stop!" Sarya shouted in Kurdish, and they stopped shooting.

"We have to get them," Barî said. "Or other teams will be in danger."

Gan he was right!

"Gulan and Olan stay here; the rest come with me."

Sarya raced down the staircase, around and around to emerge next to the cafe. The boys were about 50 metres away.

"Surrender please!" Sarya pleaded in Arabic.

"Never!" a young voice, not yet broken, shouted back while he aimed his rifle.

"Shoot them!" Sarya ordered in Kurdish, and they did. Rifle fire echoed in the street which was like a canyon, and those boys had no chance. When they were all down, the shooting stopped. Sarya ran and some were alive.

She grabbed her radio and pressed the transmit button. "Clara; Sarya. DAESH casualties downstairs from our objective," she said in Kurdish. "DAESH boys. The way's clear to get ambulances through."

"Alright Sarya," Clara said. "Ambulances coming."

Sarya squatted on her haunches and felt tears welling. Some were alive but at least three were dead. She'd heard stories from other teams and seen the toll on their faces, and now she knew.

She stood amongst her men; all clearly shocked. Stoic, as men were stoic under stress. "This is the fault of DAESH, who kidnapped these children and brainwashed them," Sarya said firmly. "DAESH did this and not us. Now we'll go upstairs and carry any other survivors down."

They nodded, and followed her up to the roof once more. There were two others still alive, and they carefully carried their little bodies down the staircase. By the time they reached the bottom, comrades from two APCs were loading survivors. One of those comrades looked up, and Sarya got the greatest shock! Barî, Keya, Soran and Sarya placed the other two boys inside, before Sarya moved away from her team.

"Leila," Sarya said. "I'm so sad to see you at such a time."

Leila put her arms out and hugged Sarya, and Sarya needed the touch of a friend. That was something she couldn't do with the men of her team or even with Gulan.

"I'm sorry for what we did," Sarya said quietly.

"I know this wasn't your fault."

"That doesn't make the hurt go away." Sarya pulled away and looked into Leila's eyes. "The Battle of Raqqah is like a journey to hell."

Leila nodded. Beside her, one of the APC drivers looked terribly shocked. Sarya went close to him.

"Look after them Havel," she said. "Leila; look after them too."

Sarya saw the driver's face change, and Leila's face change too, and what was a mission of despair became a mission of hope. Comrade drivers and Leila climbed into their vehicles, did awkward turns over rubble, and drove away. Once more that day, Sarya took a deep breath to calm wild thoughts. She then went upstairs with the men following. Someone had seen them take that building and sent those children in. Despite that tragedy they couldn't afford to relax for a moment, until they were relieved.

* * *

Vache sat exhausted in one of the two plastic chairs in their field hospital: a former grocer's shop with the roller door ripped away. Shelves behind held their medical equipment, while their faithful examination table, and table for medical implements, occupied the centre. One of SDF's home-made armoured personnel carriers rattled to a stop, and immediately Erna and their other nurses, Dila and Ajda, sprung into action. They led three casualties from the cramped rear of the APC, and one of those men was in a bad way. Vache told Dila and an accompanying soldier to bring that man to the examination table, while Erna dealt with an injured young woman soldier bleeding from a gash to her arm.

The soldier on the examination table was quite badly injured, and close to unconscious.

"Stay awake!" Vache shouted in Arabic, after noting the soldier's uniform didn't have a YPG patch.

The young soldier's head lolled.

"I'm Vache, he said. "What happened?"

"He was shot by a sniper," the accompanying soldier said.

"How long ago?"

"Maybe an hour."

Vache grimaced. It took time to get an APC to the scene of an injury, load up casualties, and get back while dealing with road blockages set up by DAESH, which was a task in itself. Drivers couldn't stop or they'd be targeted by rockets, so they cruised along while hanging out of the door and kicking blockages out of the way. All of that took too much time.

The young soldier on the table was shot in the chest, and that was dangerous. He could end up with collapsed lungs and suffocate. He was also bleeding from his arm. If only there was a hospital in Raqqah beyond field hospitals, but there wasn't. The nearest proper hospital was in Tel Abyad; about an hour and a half away.

Vache pulled on a fresh pair of latex gloves and held the soldiers wrist. Pulse was 48, which was far too low. Vache cleaned the chest wound; then wiped antiseptic before applying an ocular dressing; while knowing that wasn't enough. With such a low pulse the young soldier was bleeding internally, and stood next to no chance of surviving the long drive to Tel Abyad. Vache then tore the soldier's uniform to expose the wound in his arm. Again he cleaned the wound before wiping antiseptic; then wrapped a bandage tightly, and strapped that tighter with a tourniquet. But that wasn't going to be enough because that young soldier was going to die from his internal bleeding.

"Get a stretcher, please," Vache asked Dila in Kurdish.

She got one from an ambulance, to allow Vache and the comrade soldier to place the wounded soldier on that stretcher.

"Tell them to get this man to Tel Abyad as fast as possible," Vache told Dila. "It's important they keep him awake."

The driver and the comrade soldier rushed the wounded man to the back of the ambulance while Dila spoke with the medic. The medic climbed in, doors were slammed, and the van roared away. Vache stood and watched.

"What is it Vache?" Dila asked.

"He's going to die," Vache said flatly.

"That's tragic."

"I know." Vache drew a deep breath. "Who else do we have?"

"Havel Boznan," Dila said. "Shrapnel wound from a grenade drone."

"I'm Vache," Vache said in Kurdish to the YPG soldier. "Sit on the table, Havel Boznan."

This one was relatively straightforward, and treatable in their field hospital. Vache changed gloves before grabbing a bottle of local anaesthetic, and applying that to the wound.

"We'll wait for a few minutes," Vache told Havel Boznan.

Once the antiseptic had numbed the wound, Vache used sterilised tweezers to extract remnants of the grenade from a shallow wound; bleeding lightly. Piece by piece, metal shards rattled into a steel kidney dish, until the wound was clean. Then antiseptic and a bandage, wrapped tight.

"Keep this bandage in place for five days," Vache said. "If this is still painful after more than three days; you must return here."

Havel Boznan nodded in agreement with that instruction, and they shook hands before the young soldier left.

Erna had dealt with the young woman, so all was calm once more.

"We're doing alright," Erna said.

Vache sighed. "I know, but the only working hospital in Raqqah is controlled by DAESH."

"We save more than we lose."

That was true, and Erna being a qualified nurse made a big difference. She could deal with most injuries at a field hospital level, which was equivalent to having two doctors, along with Dila and Ajda to assist. Just then an APC rattled to a halt, and Dila, a former armourer who absolutely shone in her new role of nurse, went to help. They had to carry a wounded young YPG soldier to the examination table, and that was like the young Arab soldier all over again. Vache changed gloves and went to see what he could do; short of surgery and a blood transfusion. Erna was right; they saved more than they lost, but the battle within Raqqah was really, really tough. They saw many more casualties than any previous battles. He wondered how long it would take to defeat DAESH in this labyrinth of streets and ruined apartment buildings, just to bring the stream of casualties to an end.

The young YPG soldier was wounded in his abdomen, and it was a bad one. Vache sighed deeply, before he held the soldiers wrist to check his pulse. Maybe, just maybe, no vital organs were damaged and it looked worse than it was.

* * *

Adnan woke and went to the bathroom, where he poured water from the jug into the sink to wash his face. Wash he did, for little good. Some weeks before, their windows were smashed after an airstrike two buildings away. Their apartment was full of grit. Every surface, everything he touched, was gritty. But that was the least of their worries. Anas the grocer was able to leave, and neighbours gathered to share his stock of food equally amongst all. That stock: tinned tomatoes, tinned string beans, tinned fruit, sausages and other items, was running out. Adnan knew what he had to do after that, but he didn't really want to. He didn't want to do that.

Adnan's wash was the last of their water from yesterday, so he dressed in his DAESH-like clothes, before taking two jugs outside. There the street was already shimmering with heat, despite early morning. Adnan stopped and looked carefully, but saw or heard nothing out of the ordinary. He paused while considering why DAESH militants shot unarmed civilians. If DAESH was at war, then Kurdish soldiers were targets, but not men and women, and even old people, going out for survival. Adnan drew a deep breath and stepped into dirt and rubble, which made walking difficult. He stayed alert while looking all around, but heard nothing beyond the never ending sound of war in the background. Rifle shots, artillery, the odd missile strike; but all at a distance.

Adnan plodded on until he almost tripped, and noticed the laces on one of his shoes were untied. He put the jugs down and squatted to tie his laces, when suddenly there was a crack and a loud ricochet against the wall above his head. Dirt sprayed while Adnan ducked even lower. That was close! Adnan spotted a building where that sniper might be. If not that building then somewhere in that vicinity. While keeping low, Adnan carried his jugs to the other side of the street, where hopefully he was protected by the ruined shells of buildings. Still ducking low, Adnan carried his jugs to the end of the street where he stopped once more. There he checked, but he was in trouble because he would be in the open for a moment. Taking a deep breath, Adnan ran across the street just as he heard three shots, and bullets struck rubble to his right. Fortunately his sniper was a poor shot. But against buildings once more, he ought to be safe. He climbed over rubble on his way to the well; which was intact and hidden in an alcove. There he pumped precious water, before screwing caps tight on his jugs.

Adnan returned over rubble to the right of the street, while burdened with eight litres of water, which caused him to stumble on loose chunks of concrete. He reached the intersection with his own street, and there he paused to take a deep breath. He looked left and right, and again wondered why DAESH shot at unarmed civilians. He hoped when the Kurds came, they killed every DAESH, although DAESH would commit suicide instead. Either way, the world would be a better place without them.

Adnan sprinted across the street, but this time he wasn't shot at. When he reached the cover of buildings on his own street he paused to regain his breath, before heading home, up the stairs, and into their apartment.

"I have water," Adnan said.

"Did it go well?" Ranim asked.

"I was shot at but he missed."

Ranim sighed. "What are we to do?"

"I'm sure Kurds have dealt with mines and DAESH patrols on the roads out the city." Adnan thought about his near miss. "But we have to get to Kurdish lines, and that's like committing suicide."

They had little food, no tea, no way to cook, and Adnan wasn't in the mood for anything other than feeling sorry for himself. No reading, no card games; just moping around the apartment until it was time to eat. Ranim read a book before nagging him to do something useful, but Adnan didn't have the energy to argue with her. He sat at the table until Ranim opened the last of their tins, and they shared cold baked beans. Sometime after that he heard knocking on their door, and Adnan went to greet Nizar and Layal. Adnan let them into the apartment while Usama climbed the stairs from behind. Next were Papa Fakhri, Mama Fakhri and Saami. More and more arrived, taking spaces on the dirty couch or on dirty kitchen chairs brought into the dirty living room, while Adnan checked everyone off. They were all there which meant they'd all survived.

"Anything to report?" Usama asked.

"I was shot at this morning by a DAESH towards the end of this street," Adnan said. "If you keep to this side of the street, you'll be out of his line of sight."

Some nodded while they considered that. Every evening they met to share tips for survival; in Adnan's apartment because it was most intact.

"How's food going?" Rifat asked. He was in his 60s and the oldest, and naturally took charge of their group.

"We've nearly run out," Adnan said.

"You know what you have to do."

Adnan did, although stealing from the dead was morbid. But in apartments of those who'd perished, they would find enough to get by. "Tomorrow when I get water, I'll search for food."

"If there are bodies you can cover them with blankets, and that's a good deed."

"I will."

"Does anyone know where the Kurds are?" Ali asked.

"Close," Rifat said.

"How do you know?"

"There's been a lot of shooting to the east of here, which can only be battles between Kurds and DAESH."

"We don't want to be caught in the middle of that," Adnan said.

"No you don't," Rifat said. "Go out early to get water and search for food, and then stay inside. At best you could get caught in crossfire, but at worst DAESH may take you for a human shield."

"That would be pointless!" Adnan exclaimed. "Kurds shoot snipers or blow-up buildings regardless of human shields.'

"They have no choice."

Adnan knew Kurds had no choice, and surely DAESH knew that too. If DAESH was going to be defeated, then it was inevitable there were going to be civilian casualties. DAESH killed more civilians than Kurds anyway.

Darkness was descending, and soon it would be time for bed. Sometimes even to sleep, but only after a few sleepless nights when exhaustion took over. Any stocks of matches, and makeshift candles made out of strips of cardboard and wood, were kept for emergencies. So life was to rise from bed when the sun came up, and go to bed when the sun went down.

"We should go," Rosarita said. "Good luck to everyone."

"Good luck," Papa Fakhri said before kissing Adnan's and Ranim's cheeks, as did Mama Fakhri and Saami.

They left as did all the survivors; and all with wishes of good luck. Then they were together, alone, in their apartment. Adnan contemplated his beautiful wife, and especially her cool calmness. That calmness kept him going more than anything else.

"I love you," he said.

"I love you too," she said.

"We'll survive."

"I know."

In near darkness they went to their bedroom. In bed,
Adnan lay on his back. He remembered their best time
together; the day he moved from boyhood to manhood.
Mama hugged Adnan, and said that Ranim was a wonderful
girl who was like a daughter to her. Lina then hugged Adnan
and also said that Ranim was wonderful. Papa then said it
was time for Adnan to earn real money. As always, Adnan
felt his eyes go moist, because Lina never had that moment.
That was cruelly denied her. In the background were the
never-ending sounds of war, while Adnan was sure they
would meet again in paradise.

Chapter Twenty Four

Adnan kept to the left of the street to be out of the line of sight of that sniper, until he reached the intersection. There he peered around the corner, with war a distance away as artillery boomed and gunshots echoed. He took a deep breath and ran, but surprisingly wasn't shot at. That was odd. Keeping to the side of the street out of sight of that sniper, he climbed over rubble to the well, where he momentarily contemplated that pump miraculously surviving destruction all around. There Adnan filled his jugs before screwing two caps securely in place. He turned towards home, just a short distance away, and their neighbourhood was quiet. Very, very quiet. Adnan stopped, and took a deep breath to cross into his street when a woman's voice shouted 'stop!'. Adnan turned to see a soldier in green camouflage, pointing a rifle at him. Immediately he dropped his jugs and shot his hands into the air, while two male soldiers also aimed rifles at him.

"Who are you and what are you doing here?" she snapped.

"My name's Adnan Richie and I live here," Adnan blurted.

"You can't live here; it's too dangerous. You must go." She lowered her rifle. "You can put your hands down," she said.

Adnan did, just as the two male soldiers came to the woman soldier. They spoke in another language, almost certainly Kurdish, before the woman pointed further along the street. The men went to where she pointed, and Adnan realised she was their officer. He looked into her face and it was a young face. Younger than Ranim but with cold, hard eyes. They were the eyes of a soldier who would kill a man as soon as look at him.

"What is it?" she asked.

"Are you an officer?" Adnan asked.

"Why do you want to know? No." She slung her rifle over her shoulder and came to him. "I'm Commander Sarya of the Syrian Democratic Forces."

They shook hands.

"Now Adnan Richie; you must go."

"Is it clear to the east of here?" Adnan asked.

"If you keep behind our lines to the east, you'll be safe" Commander Sarya said "Be careful of these," she said; pointing out a plastic jug. "Any jugs or bags of rice or anything like that; could be improvised bombs, which will blow-up if you touch them."

"Then what should I do?"

"We've cleared mines from the road to Turkey. I don't know the name, but you will know which road I mean. There are trucks which will take you to Turkey for a little money. Do you have money?"

"I do," Adnan said. "I'll get my wife and we'll go."

Adnan picked up his water jugs.

"Good luck Adnan Richie," she said.

"Good luck to you, Commander Sarya."

Adnan thought he saw a small flash of a smile, before he picked his way over the rubble of their street. DAESH was gone and they could get away, and that was an important thing to know. He climbed their stairs and let himself inside, where Ranim was already dressed.

"We can leave," he said.

"Where; how," Ranim asked.

"Sorry," Adnan apologised. "A Kurdish woman soldier told me their lines are to the east of here, which means DAESH are isolated to the west. If we keep east we can get out unmolested."

"That's wonderful. What was she like?"

"Young and beautiful, but a real soldier and dangerous. She was nice when she realised I was a civilian. I have to change out of these clothes." Adnan thought. "We'll tell your family and go together."

"DAESH women wear abayas, so I'll dress casually to go through Kurdish lines. Like you I won't look DAESH."

"Good idea. Something could go wrong if Kurdish soldiers think the wrong thing."

Adnan pulled on blue trousers and a white shirt, and his black trainers once more. He packed a bag of underwear, socks, more trousers and shirts, toiletries and the bottle of water they were going to take that night. Beside him, Ranim packed her bag. She already wore dark trousers and a light-blue blouse, but then she went to the wardrobe to bring out a hijab. She pondered it.

"How did that woman soldier wear her hair?" Ranim asked.

"She had a scarf wrapped over her ponytail."

Ranim brought out a blue scarf and tied it over her ponytail; a lot like the soldier. "Like this?" she asked.

"Yes."

"I still believe in God like that soldier probably believes in God, but I don't believe in men's rules for women anymore. So no hijab."

Adnan understood. "That looks good. You're beautiful and you have lovely hair."

He watched Ranim smile brightly before she slung her backpack in place. "Let's go," she said.

For the last time they went downstairs to destruction, and around the corner at the eastern end of their street, to Ranim's family living in a semi-ruin. There they climbed stairs and knocked on the doorframe with no door. They were greeted with a look of shock by Mama Fakhri; no doubt by Ranim's casual dress.

"We're going and you're coming with us," Ranim said.

"How?" Mama Fakhri asked.

"To the east of here is clear, all the way to Turkey. Pack what you can carry, bring all the money you have, and we're going together."

"A Kurdish soldier told me," Adnan said. "Keep to the east behind Kurdish lines, and trucks will take us to Turkey for money."

"Come in, come in," Mama Fakhri said. "No abaya, no niqab, and no hijab."

"I'm a good Muslim but I can't cover up anymore," Ranim said.

"God looks into our hearts and not at what's on our heads."

Ranim nodded.

"We won't be a moment," Mama Fakhri said.

It didn't take long before Papa Fakhri, Mama Fakhri and Saami were dressed and packed for a long journey. However, Mama Fakhri dressed traditionally Syrian. They went downstairs together, and then walked east along a trail bulldozed through rubble by Kurdish forces; bustling with men and women in green camouflage carrying all varieties of weapons. For sure the defeat of DAESH was only a matter of time, but in the process most of Raqqah was destroyed. It would be many years before life returned to those ruins.

"I'm glad we made it out alive," Papa Fakhri said. "But I'm sorry for you loss."

Adnan was terribly sorry. "Of course that was tragic and of course I miss them, but we've been working hard at surviving and the only time I've had to grieve is alone at night; always with the sound of war in the background. Each time I think of them, I vow not to let their deaths be in vain. Ranim and I will survive and we'll have a family in time, with a son named Abdi and a daughter named Sarina. We'll put this tragic time behind us, and DAESH will just be a bad memory."

"Who would have thought when those demonstrations started, that this would be the outcome?"

Adnan surveyed the ruins and soldiers, and even bodies covered in blankets, and who would have thought? DAESH was able to occupy a vacuum created by the defeat of Assad's regime, until Kurds to the north saw what was happening and they fought back.

On and on they walked, being stopped by soldiers from time to time, until eventually they reached the northern outskirts of Raqqah. There was a faded blue cattle or sheep truck already with about ten on board, complete with all they could carry. A middle-aged man stood near the rear, and Adnan went to him.

"Are you taking passengers?" Adnan asked.

"Yes," the man said. "One-hundred dollars each."

"I don't have one hundred dollars each. I have one hundred dollars for the two of us."

"That's not enough," he said dismissively.

"I'll give you a choice," Adnan said. "One hundred dollars for the two of us, or nothing at all."

"Why should I accept that?"

"Because earning one hundred dollars is better than earning nothing."

He grimaced and put out his hand. Adnan handed over two notes before helping Ranim climb on board. Her family then negotiated a price based on what they had. They climbed on board, which filled the truck to capacity. Tailgate was slammed shut, cab door was slammed equally hard, engine roared into life, and they were on their way. Adnan knew the Kurdish advance was from the north to Raqqah, so driving north to Turkey was through Kurdish-held territory. It was going to be a safe drive, although he wondered what he would find at their destination.

The truck roared along the deserted highway across a flat and featureless landscape for a few hours, in intense heat with the sun beating down from a clear, blue sky. Eventually they slowed at a guardpost. There the driver spoke with uniformed officials; undoubtedly Turkish, before the white gate was raised and they were on their way but this time in Turkey. They took a road to the right, and a short time later arrived at the gate to the camp, although that camp was beyond anything Adnan could have imagined. Rows and rows of white tents stretching as far as he could see, lined neat, paved roads, within a border fence topped by razor wire. People bustled as if it were a city, which it was. A tent city for Syrian refugees. Uniformed guards slid the gate open, it too topped by razor wire, so the truck could enter.

They stopped at a portable building with airconditioner rumbling. Moments later several men and women emerged from that building, while Adnan climbed down awkwardly because his legs were somewhat cramped after sitting for so long. He helped Ranim to climb down, before grabbing their backpacks just as a young woman in a hijab came to them.

"Marhaba," she said. "My name's Ayla and welcome to Akçakale Refugee Camp.

Adnan shook her hand. "Marhaba," he said. "My name's Adnan Richie and this is my wife Ranim, and we're from Raqqah."

"You must have suffered in Raqqah these past months. A camp isn't a home, but we'll do the best we can to look after you. Here we have the facilities of a good sized city, from a hospital to schools, kindergartens, mosques, supermarkets, other shops, cinemas, gyms, and other social and leisure facilities. We'll find work for you if we can, and you'll also get a pension of eighty Turkish liras a month each. You'll get a tent with beds, blankets and sheets, and then we'll take things from there." Ayla looked at a clipboard for a moment. "Come with me," she said.

They headed into the tent city with Adnan curious. Really curious. "Who pays for this?" he asked.

"Most of the funding for this and other camps in Turkey comes from the Turkish government, who have been generous to Syrians in need."

"And you said you would find us jobs?"

"This is a city and there's always work. What work did you do?"

"I worked in a cafe."

"With luck we can find you similar work here. And you Ranim?"

"I worked for a pharmacy," Ranim said. "I sold cosmetics, hair dyes and things like that, but only until DAESH took power."

"No need to worry about DAESH here," Ayla said. "I'm sure we can find work for you too." She stopped. "This tent is free, so this is your new home."

Adnan followed Ranim inside to a canvas tent where it was possible to stand. The floor was solid and covered by a carpet; there was a cupboard and even a television set. A bed of course, with sheets, blankets and towels at the end. Blankets weren't necessary because in late summer heat, that tent was stiflingly hot.

"This is good," Adnan said.

"I'll let you get settled," Ayla said. "There's a map of the camp on the side of the cupboard, which shows where the bathroom blocks are. I'll come back tomorrow and arrange work if you want that."

She left and Ranim sat on the bed. "I can't believe this," she said. "We should have come here a long time ago."

Adnan sat beside her. "There was a brief time when we could have come here, but by the time things started going really bad, DAESH would let you out of Raqqah," he said.

She hit her forehead with the palm of her hand. "Of course! And the same for your family because of Lina."

"So without the money for bribes, we had to wait for liberation."

"Liberation only came today. We made it, but I'm sorry about your family, and I'm sorry about those who didn't make it."

"As hospitable as this is, this is still a camp surrounded by barbed wire," Adnan said.

"It'll be years before Raqqah is fit for habitation, and probably years for many other cities in Syria. We can get by here, and we can have a family now. We've waited a long time to have a family."

That was true. With a hospital, schools and everything else, they could have a family. Their future daughter can have an education, while their future son won't be brainwashed by DAESH. Adnan held Ranim's hand and looked into her eyes, and they could have a family, for which they'd waited more than five years. But it was very hot in that tent, and strangely claustrophobic despite more than enough space.

"I'm going out for fresh air," Adnan said, and he went through the flap to stand on the crushed gravel path. There were tents as far as he could see, spaced about half a metre apart, except for one metre wide paths dividing them into rows. Tents half a metre to one metre apart, for tens of thousands of refugees. Just a few metres away was the wire fence topped by razor wire, and despite hospitals and mosques, surely they were in prison as if they'd both committed heinous crimes. A prison of tents which were stifling in summer, undoubtedly freezing in winter, with some work to pass the days. For how long would they stay in that prison? That depended on what happened in Syria.

"What's wrong?" Ranim asked.

Adnan gazed at the fence topped by razor wire. "I'm not being ungrateful, but trapped behind a wire fence in a country that doesn't want us, isn't a proper life."

Ranim stood beside and stared at the fence. 'You're right," she said quietly. "We can have a family now that our children will be safe from DAESH, but I don't want our children to be raised in a camp surrounded by that fence."

Adnan pondered their future, beyond Akçakale Refugee Camp. DAESH would be defeated in Raqqah, before being defeated at their last stronghold of Dier ez Zor and surrounding countryside to there. Then what? Kurds would get an autonomous region to the north of Syria, which they deserved, and there would be democratic elections for all of Syria. Parties other than Assad's Baath parry would surely win, forming a dysfunctional coalition with conflicting views and ideas. Cities would be rebuilt, with Raqqah and Aleppo the most damaged, and life would return to something like normal.

But DAESH would still lurk. Like Iraq, terror attacks would continue, with suicide car bombs at markets, mosques and anywhere there was a crowd. To make things worse; DAESH had a ready source of suicide bombers from the thousands of boys they brainwashed at school. The death toll in Syria would grow week by week and month by month; just like Iraq. They would never see peace in their lifetimes. Why?

"The war on Iraq," Adnan said quietly. "Without that invasion by American, Britain and Australia, there would have been no DEASH, no destruction of Raqqah, we wouldn't be here, and we wouldn't be facing a future of terror attacks by DAESH once we return to Syria.

"I wonder if George Bush, Tony Blair and John Howard struggle with the suffering they caused," Ranim said. "The million who died, and more than ten million refugees."

"Thirteen and a half million refugees," Adnan said.

Ranim gasped.

"Those men wouldn't give us a second thought," Adnan said bitterly. "We'll return to Syria one day, with a family if we're lucky, but there won't be peace as we once knew it."

Adnan stared at the fence and wondered how things could have gone so wrong.

Chapter Twenty Five

Sarya stirred from her bed of a blanket on dirty concrete. Around her they slept, while Sarya wondered about the surreal nature of her existence. Advancing at night along streets lined by ruined buildings, and then taking a designated building to push their front lines ever closer to Naeem Roundabout, the Circle of Hell, and the DAESH headquarters a little further along in the National Hospital. In those newly-taken ruined buildings they camped amongst dirt and rubble until relieved by daytime forces, and then they returned to camp to eat and sleep. After they woke and ate, they passed a few hours until it was time to advance once more.

Sarya went to the gas ring. She lit it and soon had a cup of tea. By then Gulan and Olan were awake, and they poured glasses of tea as well.

"Sleep well?" Sarya asked.

Gulan nodded. "The sleep of exhaustion."

"Me too," Olan said.

The rest of their team woke, and they all poured tea.

"Whose turn is it?" Gulan asked.

"Your turn," Soran said.

"I thought so."

Gulan wandered off to the communal kitchen in the part-ruined apartment building that served as their camp.

Sarya grabbed a bottle of water and poured some into her hands to freshen her face. She rubbed herself clean after a fashion, while the others used the same bottle to wash in the same way.

In the kitchen, Gulan was dealing with their usually limited ingredients, being oil, eggs, salt, bread and yoghurt. She was frying eggs with oil over a gas ring. That was served onto paper plates, along with bread on a plate, and a tub of yoghurt with a spoon. That was a good meal to start the afternoon. It had taken time to get used to the back-to-front routine of advancing at dusk into night, and consolidating during daylight hours. Back-to-front it was, but it worked better. There were less sniper and machine gun attacks, although grenade drones and suicide cars remained hazards.

Other advance teams stirred and joined them in the kitchen. Sarya greeted comrades in either Kurdish or Arabic, depending on which arm patches they wore. There were fewer women than men in teams actually pushing the front line, although there were some. Sarya noticed an aura from those women, of ability and confidence that came from experience. Sarya guessed other women would sense similar in Gulan and she.

Just then Sarya heard women's voices, and looked up to see five women, including Medya wearing a cap like Barî's cap! Sarya could believe it! Sarya went to Medya, whose eyes were wide with shock. Sarya grabbed her friend and kissed her cheeks.

"It's wonderful to see you," Sarya said.

"It's wonderful to see you," Medya said. "Are you still with your team?"

"Sarya's our commander," Gulan said.

Medya's eyes were even wider when she kissed Gulan's cheeks. "You're on the front line too," she said to Gulan.

"And you're still a sniper?"

"I am. And Komutan Sarya!"

"That's nothing," Sarya said dismissively. "I'm just proud to be part of the best team in the SDF, and playing my part in the defeat of DAESH."

"Me too," Medya said. "Sometimes it's hard, especially here, but I always remember I'm playing my part."

"How do you do it?" Sarya asked.

"These past two days I've been on a plastic chair in a little room, staring through a hole punched through a concrete wall while waiting for my target."

Sarya was amazed. "For two days?" she gasped.

"When it got dark I slept, and then I woke again. But I got him, and that's one less for you to worry about."

Sarya was still amazed.

"The village battles weren't so bad," Medya said. "They used us because we have the right rifles for long-range shots. Here is hard though."

"Here is hard for all of us," Gulan said. "But soon this will be over."

Medya looked thoughtful. "One part of me wants this to be over," she said. "Another part of me doesn't want to go back just to be a wife and a mother. I've touched it now, and I can't give it up."

"I'm going to study at university to be a doctor," Sarya said.

"How?"

"It's five years at university, and the doctor here is going to help me."

"You're lucky."

"You could study at university."

"Five years is a long time to...," Medya said while looking at the dirty concrete floor. "Five years is a long time to wait."

Sarya guessed what Medya was trying to say, and she'd already thought about that. When in those villages with time to think about how she felt. "I'm not going to wait," she said firmly. "If I can fight in this war like a man, then I can do other things like a man."

Medya nodded thoughtfully. "Then I will study; but I'm not so sure about five years."

Sarya thought about Erna. "The doctor has a nurse who works with him. She has a lot of medical knowledge and I'm sure she's studied, but not for five years."

Gulan nodded. "If not a doctor then a nurse?" she offered.

"Dila is a nurse these days," Medya said.

Sarya was surprised. "Really?" she exclaimed.

"Dila is here in Raqqah and happy to be helping wounded comrades." Medya looked into Sarya's eyes. "To be a doctor or a nurse is more than just a job."

Sarya knew that. "We'll all be back in Amûdê, God willing," she said. "The doctor and nurse, Vache and Erna, will contact me there, and they can advise us; including Dila if she wants."

"That's good," Medya said. "No, that's great." Her team, possibly a group of snipers, were preparing their meal. "I must go," Medya said.

"Is your team all women?" Sarya asked.

"Yes. Women make better snipers because we have more patience to wait for the right shot."

Sarya smiled brightly at that. Not only were women equal in war; they were better! "We women are as good as men, and sometimes better, and we've shown that."

Medya kissed Sarya's cheeks. "We are, Komutan Sarya."

Sarya hugged Medya.

"You brought us all here," Medya whispered in her ear.

Sarya remembered.

Sarya let Medya go, and Gulan kissed Medya's cheeks.

"We'll meet in Amûdê, God willing," Gulan said. "There we have the rest of our lives to plan for."

"We do my dear friends," Medya said, before joining her team.

Sarya watched them together, before returning to their sleeping space under a suspended staircase.

"A friend?" Soran asked.

"A school friend who volunteered with us," Sarya said. "It's good to know she's survived."

"Soon this will be over."

Sarya knew that victory was near; even if the Battle of Raqqah was tougher than she ever imagined war could be. Mina once warned her and Mina was absolutely right.

"Your bet is going to come true," Olan said. "This'll be over by the middle of next month. Syrian DAESH have deserted and only foreign fanatics remain. How many do you think?"

"Maybe four-hundred," Sarya said.

"Do you know or think?"

"I know other teams think four-hundred."

"I never would have believed this would be over by mid-October," Barî said.

"We're too good!" Soran exclaimed.

"But there's nothing left of Raqqah! Almost all of the city's been destroyed!"

"Did you study World War Two at school?" Sarya asked.

"No."

"This is seventy years ago, and almost every city in Germany, Poland and parts of Russia were destroyed as badly as here, and cities in other countries too. Yet in ten years, Germany was the most productive country in Europe, while Poland, Russia and all those other countries were rebuilt. It's devastated out there, but it will come back."

"There's a reason why we study history at school," Gulan said.

"I understand," Barî said.

Strangely, they talked about war and history for a few hours, and strangely that made everyone feel better. Until the afternoon faded, and Sarya led their team to Clara, who gave Sarya a tablet computer.

"Coordinate fourteen-eleven," she said.

"Thanks Clara," Sarya said.

"Look after yourself."

"You know me."

"I know you all, and I don't want to lose any of you!" Clara exclaimed.

"We'll be fine," Keya said.

"I know you will. Good luck."

They headed into the dusk, along a path bulldozed through rubble, towards coordinate 1411.

Vache bound the wound on the young, Arab soldier's arm, and got him to stand.

"You'll be fine, Comrade," Vache said in Arabic. "Avoid using that arm for the next two or three days; so no shooting rifles."

"Alright Doctor," the young soldier said, before he walked away.

Vache relaxed in one of the two plastic chairs in their field hospital. Just then voices approached with a man protesting in Kurdish that he was alright. A woman told him quite firmly that the doctor was going to check his wound, and Vache knew who that was. There they were: Sarya with Keya from her team. Sarya nodded in acknowledgement but her eyes were flat and glazed, like all soldiers in the Battle of Raqqah.

"Silav Vache," she greeted in Kurdish.

"Silav Sarya," Vache replied in Kurdish. "What do we have here?"

"A grenade drone went off and Keya was hit with debris."

"Keya; can you sit on the table please?"

Keya sat. Vache checked the wound on his leg, through his torn, polyester uniform.

"Sarya's right," Vache said. "We'll clean this, bind it, and you'll be right. If we don't treat you; this could get infected, and then you'll be in trouble."

Keya nodded.

"Erna; can you clean and dress this please?" Aria asked.

Erna told Keya to remove his trousers, which he did.

"How are you?" Vache asked Sarya, and she shrugged her shoulders. "Would you like a mug of coffee?"

"Coffee!" she exclaimed. "How do you always have coffee?"

"My secret. Erna; we're going upstairs for a few minutes."

She nodded. Vache took Sarya to the doorway next to the shop, and up to the ruined apartment they called home. Into their room, which had the usual mattresses on the floor, two plastic chairs, and a gas ring and cauldron. Vache struck a match and asked Sarya to sit. Soon they had coffee.

"How are you really?" Vache asked.

"I'm tired," Sarya sighed. "I'm tired of sleeping on dirty concrete, I'm tired of eating awful food, I'm tired of always looking over my shoulder, I'm tired of killing DAESH terrorists; I'm tired of the smell of death."

Vache wasn't at all surprised, given what she must have been through. He was tired of endlessly treating injured and dying men and women with facilities not up to that, and he was tired of sending men and women away to die when he wished he could save them. And he was tired of the stench of death that hung over Raqqah like a pall. Vache contemplated the porcelain mug in his hands. "Doctor prescribes a week at home in a soft bed with clean sheets, and breakfast of freshly baked bread with honey, and a cup of coffee."

"I'll do that, when Raqqah's taken."

"When will that be?"

She shrugged her shoulders. "Soon," she said quietly. "October seventeen. I have a bet."

"Are we on target for that?"

"We'll come close. How are you and Erna?"

"As long as brave men and women are fighting the worst barbarians for a generation, we'll play our parts."

"I know you will. Remember Rojava."

"I still have your father's address."

"Good."

Sarya drank her coffee, and put her mug on the floor. "Thank you Vache, and that coffee will keep me going for a few more days. Now I must round up Keya, because we need to rest."

Sarya headed downstairs, while Vache tried to imagine what she'd been through these past years. But that was beyond his imagination. She was tired and she looked it. One thing in her favour; Kurds were tough like Armenians were tough. Young Sarya would get by; he knew that.

Chapter Twenty Six

Sarya knelt on the dusty roof, looking towards the DAESH sniper's position. Olan fired the PK one shot at a time, with Gulan feeding the ammunition belt. Barî, Keya and Soran contributed with their rifles, but it was obvious their target was just out of range, even for the PK. Sarya looked for a building closer to the sniper, but they were all half-destroyed and unable to be used. Only this house was intact enough, but it was just out of range. Just then Sarya sensed movement. She looked across the roof to the upstairs rooms of the house, where she saw three figures in semi-darkness. Keeping low out of habit, Sarya sprinted across a roof littered with spent cartridge cases. There she faced a YPG comrade, and two men wearing camouflage with body-armour and beige vests; no doubt with 'press' on their backs. One of those men held a professional-looking camera.

"Rojbash Havel," Sarya greeted the comrade.

"Rojbash Komutan Sarya," he replied. "I have Daniel and Brett from Vice Television."

Sarya shook hands with Daniel, and then with Brett the cameraman. "Do you speak English?" she asked in English.

"We do," Daniel said.

"Okay," Sarya said while she gathered her thoughts. "We have a DAESH sniper under fire, but he's just out of range so I was going to call an airstrike. Come with me and I will show you."

Sarya led the way towards the parapet, and knelt beside Olan still firing.

"The DAESH sniper is there," she said while she pointed out his building. "I will call for the strike, and we will keep firing so the sniper won't get suspicious and leave his building."

Daniel nodded while Sarya told Olan what she was going to do. He nodded while he kept at one shot after the next. Sarya sat cross-legged on the dirty roof and took the tablet computer out of its cover.

"This tablet has a satellite image of all DAESH positions, real time," Sarya said. She used her fingers to zoom the image and centre it. "We are here," she said while the cameraman filmed over her shoulder. "The DAESH sniper is there. Now I will call for the airstrike." She pulled her radio from her sleeve pocket and pressed the transmit button. "Komutan Sarya Goran from Team Martyr Agir," she said in Kurdish. "Airstrike on DAESH sniper, coordinate seventeen-twelve," she said.

"Airstrike on DAESH sniper, coordinate seventeen-twelve," the operator confirmed.

Sarya put her radio away, and moments later heard the roar of a jet closing. She stood to watch while the cameraman filmed the jet flying low and fast, until the aircraft suddenly climbed vertically, straight up into the sky.

Moments later there was a massive explosion, and the sniper's position was obliterated by a cloud of concrete dust. The rest of the team celebrated, while Sarya told Daniel they got the sniper. The cloud of dust and debris slowly cleared to reveal a heap of rubble and smashed concrete. Nobody could have survived that.

"This is a good outcome," Sarya said in English to Daniel.

"How many are left?" Daniel asked.

"Maybe four-hundred," Sarya said. "But they will fight to the last." She slid her tablet into its cover, and slipped her trusty AK47 over her shoulder. "Now we must go. There's another sniper in the next street. Perhaps this time we will get him with our rifles." Olan already had the PK over his shoulder, while Gulan was burdened with the RPG and her backpack. Barî, Keya and Soran were also ready.

Daniel shook Sarya's hand. "Thank you so much, Commander Sarya," he said.

She nodded while the cameraman, Brett, shook her hand.

Sarya led their team into the three-storey house, very dark after the intense sunlight outside, down the stairway, and outside to a dirty, dusty street. She trudged over rubble while looking out for IEDs and grenade drones, and sensing the camera filming from behind.

Chapter Twenty Seven

Vache stood with Erna on the second floor of a shell of a building above Naeem Roundabout. There, joyous soldiers of the Syrian Democratic Forces drove a tank around the roundabout, in imitation of the victory lap of that roundabout by the Free Syrian Army, Jabhat al-Nusra and Islamic State, on the 6th of March, 2013. And now on October 17, 2017; what was left of Raqqah was liberated from barbarity and oppression. Amidst the ruins, the Syrian Democratic Forces celebrated. In the middle of that was Komutan Rojda Felat, flanked by Kurdish men and women under her command, with some holding big YPG, YPJ and SDF flags. Felat, a slightly built woman, grabbed the massive, yellow, SDF flag and did a lap of honour of the roundabout, with a flag bigger than she. That was a great photo opportunity for journalists there.

Vache searched through the seething mass of green camouflage, where he spotted four men and a woman holding a tall and slim, young woman aloft. She was laughing wildly, which was far removed from when Vache last saw her. He squeezed Erna's hand while he pointed the team out, and she smiled brightly. Komutan Sarya had a special place in the hearts of everyone who knew her.

"What now my love?" Erna asked.

Good question. "For now let's enjoy the celebration, because we're part of this," Vache said. "For more than three years now."

"Three years is a long time, and we have a future to consider."

That was true. "Sarya suggested Rojava, and that could be home for us."

"As honorary Kurds," Erna said with a big smile.

"We love these people, but we can be Armenian and Christian in Rojava."

"That was why Sarya suggested Rojava."

That was why Sarya suggested Rojava.

"Are we finished with war?" Erna asked.

"I think so," Vache said. "The SDF are waging the last campaign against DAESH at Dier ez Zor, and they have enough volunteers for that. Raqqah really took it out of me."

"Me too. So Rojava it is."

So Rojava it will be.

"DAESH isn't finished," Erna said.

Vache knew that. He knew there would be suicide attacks for many, many years. But life went on, and after devoting more than three years to one of the most worthy conflicts in human history, it was time for the rest of their lives. He held the hand of his wonderful wife, with who he had the honour to share the past three years of tragedy and triumph. In the end goodness overcame hate, and that was worth celebrating.

www.ingramcontent.com/pod-product-compliance
Lightning Source LLC
Chambersburg PA
CBHW070304260626
47160CB00003B/702